Stranger
Here Below

Also by Joyce Hinnefeld

In Hovering Flight

Tell Me Everything and Other Stories

Stranger Here Below

JOYCE HINNEFELD

UNBRIDLED BOOKS

This is a work of fiction. The names, characters, places and incidents are
either the product of the author's imagination or are used fictitiously,
and any resemblance to actual persons living or dead, business
establishments, events, or locales is entirely coincidental.

Unbridled Books

Library of Congress Cataloging-in-Publication Data

Hinnefeld, Joyce.
Stranger here below / Joyce Hinnefeld.
p. cm.
ISBN 978-1-60953-004-4
1. Women college students—Fiction.   2. African American women—Fiction.
3. College teachers—Fiction.   4. Berea College—Fiction.   5. Shakers—Fiction.
6. Kentucky—History—20th century—Fiction.   I. Title.
PS3558.I5448S77 2010
813'.54—dc22
2010023438

ISBN 978-1-60953-004-4

1   3   5   7   9   10   8   6   4   2

BOOK DESIGN BY SH · CV

First Printing

For Anna

I am a stranger here below,
And what I am 'tis hard to know;
I am so vile, so prone to sin,
I fear that I'm not born again.

When I experience call to mind,
My understanding is so blind—
All feeling sense seems to be gone,
Which makes me think that I am wrong.

· "The Pilgrim's Song," William Walker's Southern
Harmony and Musical Companion, No. 106

Love is a naked shadow
On a gnarled and naked tree.

· Langston Hughes, "Song for a Dark Girl"

Contents

Stranger
Here Below

Pilgrim and Stranger
1968

In April of 1968 Maze Jansen Whitman wrote a letter to her friend Mary Elizabeth Cox. She'd written many letters to Mary Elizabeth, always signing them "Sending my love, and wishing you'd come back, Maze." But Maze wrote this letter imagining it would be the last one she'd send to Mary Elizabeth, her friend since the two had met as first-year college roommates in the fall of 1961.

"It's hard to keep up with you, M. E.," the letter began, "especially when you don't respond to my letters." And it continued:

> I'm glad you've let me know where you are, at least. I guess I've stopped imagining that you'll ever come back here to Kentucky.
>
> But don't you miss us, even a bit? If not us, if not me, then maybe at least the green and lovely and godforsaken land, as Dr. Wendt used to call it? Remember him, M. E.? And remember all those hikes you and I took on Saturday mornings, the way we

ran full speed down Fat Man's Misery and slid on the rocks and laughed so hard we couldn't breathe?

But now everyone is gone, not only you. Sister Georgia dead and buried, Sarabeth and Phil gone to Canada. And Daniel, too. He is dead, M. E., killed in the war.

It's just Harris and me and our children left now. Even my mama's moved back to Torchlight, with Uncle Shade. Harris and I have twin sons, born one month ago, and I am weepy all the time. Marthie is four, and too serious already, because of me, I'm sure. I am tired and weepy and afraid all the time, not because I have two little babies but because my babies are boys. Because of what our fine nation does with its boys. They are Harris's and my children, and they are not expendable, and I do not know what to do about that.

I'm too young for all these regrets. I regret that we didn't talk Daniel out of going when we found out he'd enlisted. That Sister Georgia didn't live to know our twins. And that you have drifted farther and farther away from me and have never told me why.

I've asked myself over and over what I might have done. If it was what happened that night I stayed at your house in Richmond. Or when I came to Chicago. I thought our friendship would last, M. E., no matter all the things that got in our way. But maybe you've been trying to tell me I was wrong.

There's one thing I do want you to know, and that's our twins' names, Pilgrim and Stranger (we usually call him Ranger). They are named for you and me, for the way I remember us when we first knew each other at Berea, the way we felt when we climbed those green hills and sang those old hymns at the top of our lungs.

I hope you are happy in New York.

The letter was signed, simply, "Maze."

Sister

1872 · 1908

Georginea Fenley Ward was born in Lexington, Kentucky, in March of 1872—in the midst of an unexpected spring blizzard, when the Kentucky bluegrass was covered in white, really not itself, and the doctor could not get there in time.

Her father, Davis Ward, had insisted that her mother, Rose, spend the last month of her pregnancy at the home of her sister Lenora, outside Lexington. But he had not accompanied Rose there, planning to arrive only in time for the birth of their first child, because he wished to spend as little time as possible in the home of his brother-in-law, whose life habits (the drinking of whiskey and, earlier, the holding of slaves, to name but two) were distasteful to him.

And so, in the midst of the ruthless ice and blowing drifts, both the doctor and little Georginea's father failed to arrive in time for her birth or for her mother's death a few minutes later. Georginea's Aunt Lenora continued, throughout her life, to insist that Rose glanced at her infant daughter and faintly smiled before closing her eyes a final time on that March morning—a story that the girl Georginea and later the woman Georgia knew could not be true; she was left, she was sure, in a corner while all eyes and ears were turned toward her dying mother—Georginea herself clean and warm and tended to, always, but also completely alone.

At the age of three, long weaned from the wet nurse who came regularly to her Aunt Lenora's home through the first year of her life, she arrived at the Cincinnati home of her father, minister of the Second Presbyterian Church. Already she was a serious and dutiful child. But she was also capable, when provoked by a perceived slight, of sudden flashes of temper that flummoxed the series of nurses who cared for her until she turned twelve. There was nothing to be done, Reverend Ward told each nurse in turn; as he repeatedly observed to Georginea herself, she had inherited the steely will of her grandfather Ephraim Ward—a locally renowned abolitionist, a friend and, for a time, a fellow student of Lyman Beecher and Theodore Weld at the radical Lane Seminary.

By the age of twelve, left alone to read in her father's study for long periods, she had devised her own particular system of signs and symbols. It was a system shaped by random influences: one German nurse's fear of cats; the reading material—mostly theological treatises, with a smattering of poetry—available to her in her father's study; her father's own hunched, black-coated back as he walked stiffly from their home to his church. These became, somehow, the hot, fulsome smell of an animal's breath, connected obscurely with sexual depravity. The slow and regular ticking of a clock and a sleeping person's noisy breathing—signaling blood, and shame and dread. A gaunt man whose black hat, caught on a gust of wind, is transformed into a crow, that filthy, laughing menace. Carrion feeder. Roadside taunter. Interrupter of dreams.

At sixteen, she packed her bag, her books, and her system of symbols and left for Oberlin College. The days of the "raving Bloomerites," the outspoken women who smoked cigarettes and debated the issues of the day as if they were men, may have ended at Oberlin, but there were freedoms there that Georginea could not have imagined in the camphor-drenched shadows of her father's house. Still, she would not have expected to fall in love with a young black man. Yet there she was, by the end of her second year: in love with Tobias Jewell, toffee-skinned and brown-eyed, filled with spiritual and other passions, and possessor of the purest tenor voice the college choir had ever had.

To her shock and deep dismay, her father—son of the abolitionist Ephraim Ward, firm promoter of racial uplift in his sermons—forbade Georginea to marry him.

"God's will, Georginea, is *not* for the physical mingling of the races," he told her one spring morning in his study. Greenish-gray storm clouds brewed outside the window, and she knew she was not mistaken in thinking that his mouth curled with a kind of horror, a deep distaste, something sour and threatening there in the room between them, as he said it. With that she was removed from Oberlin and sent to the woods of Kentucky to be a teacher at a school he knew of there.

She was younger than many of her students, and she lived among the girls and young women in Ladies Hall. On her bed the day she arrived lay a copy of the student manual. "Throw back your shoulders and take a deep breath every time you step out doors. Make 500 gymnastic movements to start the blood and waken every muscle when you rise. Take a good drink of water in the middle of the forenoon, middle of afternoon, and before going to bed. Wear no fine clothing which could make you conspicuous, or make class-mates envious, or which you cannot afford."

Elsewhere in the manual students were warned against burning gunpowder or keeping firearms; such weapons were, for the duration of the academic term, to be deposited with the principal of the institution. Georginea was in a foreign land.

And yet it was, in certain ways, like Oberlin; her fellow teachers were God-fearing, in love with learning, quiet and respectful yet passionate about the future of the Union. And in 1890, the year she arrived at Berea College, on the frayed, western edges of the mountains—somewhere between the placid, rolling bluegrass she remembered from her childhood and a harsher, mountainous world to the east—over half of the 350 students enrolled there were black. They were the sons, and in a few cases the daughters, of freed slaves, former soldiers and survivors of the war, and they studied and sang and lived among white students from the mountains.

The ragged, frontier quality of the town and the newness of the school—so removed from the world she'd known in her father's stately house in Cincinnati or her Aunt Lenora's lavish rooms in Lexington—pleased Georginea. Dormitory life suited her, too; the stark simplicity of her bed, with its thin mattress and rough sheets, her nearly empty wardrobe, desk, and chair, made her feel light as air. In this clean, white, airy room she forgot, at least for a time, the heavy nights and mornings of the summer before, the blinding headaches she'd experienced in her father's house, the listlessness of her last days there.

Down the hill, on the edges of the town, gunshots often rang out. Deathly drunken brawls were common, and sometimes men—both black and white—were killed. Not far outside Berea, along Scaffold Cane Road, children nearly froze to death in the winter. Georginea would hear about such things from Lottie Johnson, the slow, heavy girl who distributed the mail in Ladies Hall and whose narrow, red-rimmed eyes grew large as she re-counted one lurid scene after another, forcing Georginea to listen to yet another whispered account of the latest gossip from "down below the tracks" before relinquishing that morning's mail.

If Kentucky was still a frontier state, home to outlaws and renegades, and if those who lived in the surrounding hills and val-leys guarded their cabins with guns near their bedsides, Georginea was barely aware of it. Vigilante gangs passed along Main Street from time to time, but Georginea, having a few yards of home-spun measured and cut at Coyle's Store or dodging the crowd of horse-drawn wagons on a Saturday morning as she crossed the muddy street, hardly noticed them. In all likelihood she would have known nothing at all of the life outside the college walls (she seldom read the local newspapers, feeling more and more detached from the world outside her own mind), had she not been pulled from her room on occasion by several of her devoted students.

These young women loved to tease her, too, about the obvious interest of another young teacher, Lowell Wesley, who had come to Berea from the mountains of Virginia. He taught mathematics, and he had arrived at the school shortly after Georginea, in the fall of 1900. He had what she considered an affected air and a ridiculous accent, but she tried at first to return his interest. Until, one darkening evening after a walk over the college grounds, he pushed her roughly against the shadowy back wall of Ladies Hall and pressed his wet lips and mustache against her mouth, his tongue prodding her teeth. She pushed him away and hurried to the building's back door, shocked to realize that some part of her had wanted, for just a moment, to return his ardor. To let his tongue in through her clenched teeth.

As the door closed behind her, she heard the yowling of a cat. After that she avoided Lowell Wesley, who never invited her to walk with him after dinner again.

When she returned to Cincinnati for the week between Christmas and the New Year, Georginea found herself plagued by a vague, nameless anxiety. Though her father was eager to learn about her work at Berea, and their conversations were polite and respectful, if distant, by the second night of her visit, her headaches had returned. At night she slept fitfully, her dreams crowded with feverish images—a hissing cat on the windowsill, the smell of its breath invading her room. A smell transformed, eventually, into the scent of her own body on Tobias's hand where he had touched her. He appeared suddenly and unexpectedly in her dreams, and she reached for him with a pained hunger. But just as suddenly he would turn his back to her, deaf to her pleading, dressed now in the black coat and hat her father wore, walking away from her, from her need, her weakness, her woman's scent.

Back at Berea after the holiday, the dreams and the headaches persisted. For hours she lay in her room in Ladies Hall, drifting between dream-laced sleep and anxious wakefulness, staring at the ceiling. When something scratched at her window she barely turned her head, certain it was a hissing, yellow-eyed cat. Or an angry crow, roused from slumber in a crook of the giant sugar maple outside Ladies Hall. At prayers in the morning after nights like these, she wept silently, wiping her tears as discreetly as possible but still giving rise to rumors and whisperings about Miss Ward's strange devotion, the depth of her religion.

Years passed, and Georginea's memories dimmed—Tobias Jewell's eyes and his sweet tenor voice slowly fading, growing blurry in her mind. Everything blurred as a new century began and attitudes at Berea began to shift, and Georginea moved through her days in a kind of fog. Her headaches persisted, along with her tearful prayers. Her sense of something having gone awry, having failed terribly—failure and disappointment in the very air she breathed—grew into a conviction: The failure was her own.

By the spring of 1908, the college had chosen to comply with a state law called the Day Law that forbade integrated education.

It was that or economic collapse, the president insisted, and so a separate school, the Lincoln Institute, was founded for black students, and Berea turned its attention to the white "children of the mountains."

At first a few other faculty members besides Miss Ward engaged in clandestine defiance of the Day Law. A cooperating staff member would turn off the lights shortly before a lecture was to begin, and when a student rose, at the instructor's leisurely request, to turn them on again, two or three formerly enrolled black students would have appeared at the back of the room. The instructor would proceed with that day's class, pretending not to notice their presence. In the early days of the Day Law, when the school's administrators were more willing to turn a blind eye, such acts were common enough.

Eventually, though, such acts could lead to a teacher's quick dismissal. Georginea knew this. Yet gradually, reading Blake and Byron into the wee hours of the night, sleeping and waking, floating between faint images of Tobias's face and of an angry, white-haired God, of swinging corpses and of somber, black-hatted men, she came to realize something very simple. They were all, beginning with her father and on through Berea's present administrators and many of its teachers, wrong. For nearly twenty years she had been their willing tool. But that would change now. They had left her no choice. The black-coated men, the dreams and blinding headaches. Tobias's sweet face and voice, slipping away from her like a quiet stream.

And so one April morning, she walked into the classroom and said loudly, "Leave the lights on, Winerip," to the old Berea groundskeeper. To the young man and woman, Winerip's son and daughter, waiting stealthily in the hallway, she said, "Come in now, no need to wait for cover of darkness; we will no longer pretend in my classroom that we honor the laws of a decadent land." It was Byron whom she quoted to begin the day's lesson.

"'On with the dance!'" she intoned, eyes blazing and cheeks inflamed, as two male faculty members arrived to escort her from her classroom. "'Let joy be unconfin'd!'" And as they grasped her arms and pulled her toward the hallway she called back over her shoulder, "'No sleep till morn, when Youth and Pleasure meet!'" She could barely make out the gaping mouths and staring eyes of the rows of students at her back, but she caught a glimpse of Winerip's daughter, smiling. And weak and feverish and frightened as she felt then, something in that smile unleashed a cold, reckless wind, blinding white sunlight warming her face as they reached the open doorway, and Miss Georginea Ward left her last class at Berea College smiling and laughing. Like a madwoman, the students in her class that day would later say.

Pilgrim and Stranger

1961

At first Maze thought Berea College might be the way Sister Georgia remembered it—a place to read and study and weave amid the towering oak trees. Solid brick buildings filled with books and music in the middle of a land of hardscrabble farms and sharecroppers' shacks. A kind of island at the smoothed-out edges of Kentucky's eastern knobs, not yet given over to horses and their wealthy owners. Someplace different from the rest of the state.

At first she'd thought that. Here, for instance, was her roommate, Mary Elizabeth Cox—a Negro girl. Shy and prickly, eyeing Maze warily, not ready to trust her, assuming the worst. But that was all right with Maze; edgy, mistrustful women were about the only kind she'd known. Sister Georgia, the woman Maze's mama, Vista, cared for, was "a mountain of mistrust," Vista said. Took one to know one, Maze might have told her mama. Now the two of them were back in Shakertown without her. Who would protect Vista and Georgia from each other? Maze had wondered many times since she'd agreed to enroll at Berea College in the fall of 1961. That was for them to figure out now. Two mountains facing off.

Most of Maze's first day at Berea had in fact been ridiculous. Miserable and ridiculous. Everyone—her mama, Mary Elizabeth's parents—so nervous and polite. It will be better when they're gone, Maze thought, and it was. Mary Elizabeth's mama and daddy left first, and after Maze finally walked Vista back to her car, she came back into their room and met her roommate's uncertain eyes with a roll of her own, and then they both laughed with relief. And Maze thought—in fact, she said—"Well, that's better." And Mary Elizabeth laughed again.

Not that it was easy at first. Over and over Maze tried to remind herself, you don't have to speak aloud every little thought you're thinkin', girl. Lord.

But it seemed she couldn't stop herself. When Mary Elizabeth played something classical and unfamiliar on the piano for her that evening, Maze asked to hear some hymns, saying, "You don't have to work so hard to impress me." Then later, back in their room: "Your mama is a beautiful woman. I love the name Sarah." And when this brought no response: "You look like her, but your eyes aren't near as sad."

Too much news too fast from the mind and heart of Miss Maze Jansen, she heard in her head then. "You need to put a lid on it once in a while, Maze," her mama had told her more than once.

But Mary Elizabeth surprised her that evening when she finally turned to answer her. "How do you know I'm not just as sad?"

That was all she needed. "Well, I'm not sayin' *you* aren't sad. That's somethin' I wouldn't know yet, of course. I'm just sayin' your eyes don't have the same sad look your mama's eyes do. All I said was what I saw. And anyway, I'd imagine your mama's lived long enough to have more to be sad about than you have. My mama sure has." At this Maze finally caught a reaction, a fleeting glance, from the other girl. Was she curious? Angry?

"I mean, she's got a good bit more to be sad about than I do," Maze went on. She thought Mary Elizabeth might ask "Like what?" But she only looked at her for a moment longer, then went back to unpacking her boxes and suitcases.

The next day was hot by seven in the morning, as they walked to the dining hall for breakfast. A full day of "get-acquainted activities" with the other new students nearly convinced Maze to call Vista and beg her to come take her home. Not that she would have done it.

Maze stayed close to Mary Elizabeth whenever she could. After lunch she tried to persuade her to duck out of the big assembly on "God's Will for the Freshman Class" and walk into town, but Mary Elizabeth only stared at her like she'd suggested they go off to commit a murder. So she closed her eyes through the long, boring speeches by the college president, then a mess of deans, and took herself someplace else in her mind—first to Berea the way it must have been seventy years before, when Georgia had first arrived; then to the edge of Shawnee Run Creek, at the end of the trail behind the Sisters' Shop, on a first warm day of spring. Three different people, Mary Elizabeth among them, nudged her to try to make her open her eyes. But she ignored them all.

After dinner that night, Maze dragged Mary Elizabeth away from the social with the faculty to a grand piano she'd seen in another room, a kind of formal lounge, down the hall. "Play for me again," she begged.

Mary Elizabeth pulled her arm free and stared hard at Maze. "You are one strange girl," she said.

That stung a bit, and Maze thought, I thought she was different, but she might be like the others. "You aren't the first person to tell me that," she answered, thinking only, *Please.* Please don't be like them. It was clear to Maze by the second day of freshman orientation that Berea College was as full of people who would find her peculiar as her high school in Harrodsburg had been. "I reckon that's why you're stuck with me," she added.

Mary Elizabeth stared at her for a while, then opened her mouth as if she were about to say something but abruptly closed it. She turned to the piano, closed her eyes, then lifted her hands to the keys. She paused for a moment, just long enough to tell Maze that this time she'd play something by Debussy, one of the *Images*, and Maze, who'd learned a little French in high school, recognized the accuracy of her accent. Then her fingers came down so lightly, like two feathers floating free from a featherbed, that Maze was surprised by the rich, echoing tones that came from within the piano's depths.

When she finished playing, her eyes were closed, her face softer than Maze had yet seen it; there were tears in her eyes when she opened them and looked over at Maze. She smiled shyly and looked down.

"Debussy's French," she said, then shrugged. "It's different when I play the French composers for some reason. I mean, *I'm* different. . . ." She shrugged again. "It's hard to explain."

"I've never heard anything like that," Maze said, surprised by how quiet her voice was. She truly never had. She shook her head and looked down. "I guess that was silly, me askin' for church music last night," she said, then looked up to meet Mary Elizabeth's eyes. "I don't know what to say when I hear something like that."

Mary Elizabeth smiled at her. "Well, that's a first," she said, and they both laughed. "And it's okay; I do play a lot of church music, too," and before Maze could answer she started in on "Will the Circle Be Unbroken?" At the last "by and by" Maze interrupted her to say, "If you don't mind, I'd like to hear you play some more Debussy." She wondered, when she said it, if she'd pronounced it right.

If she was wrong, Mary Elizabeth didn't correct her. "All right," she said, lifting her fingers from the keys and stretching them out in all directions a few times. "I'll play some pieces from *The Children's Corner*," she said. "I worked and worked on these when I was younger, with my aunt. She loved Debussy. He wrote these for his daughter. This one's called 'Dr. Gradus ad Parnassum.'"

While Mary Elizabeth played, Maze closed her eyes and leaned back into her chair and tried to imagine the life of a child in Paris, France. But the more she listened, the more she found herself dreaming of her own childhood, of happy summer days along the creek, of the rhythm of the loom as Georgia held her on her lap, her feet pumping the pedals and her big, gnarled hands guiding Maze's own small ones.

When, after the slow, fading notes at the end of "The Snow Is Dancing," a security guard came to lock up the building and shooed them out of the lounge, Maze opened her eyes and looked at the clock, shocked to realize it was eleven o'clock. Their classes would begin the next day. This time she was the one with tears in her eyes.

I f she'd just looked more closely, she might not have misjudged Maze so, Mary Elizabeth often thought later when she relived that first day. She also might not have wasted time trying to play the Brahms Intermezzo—a piece she hadn't yet mastered and in truth didn't much like—and instead gotten right to the works she loved. When she finished playing that first night and looked over at Maze, she watched as the girl breathed in and then out, deep and slow. She noticed her freckles then; before that she'd been too distracted by the uncontrollable waves of Maze's reddish-blond hair, kinkier even than her own since she'd begun to straighten it years before.

And of course then Maze had done what Mary Elizabeth expected her to do; she'd asked for hymns, or for some country tune. But there was the other thing she'd said then, too: "You don't have to try to impress me." She'd known what Mary Elizabeth was up to. But then she tried to take it back. She nearly tripped over herself trying to undo what she'd done. She could not close her mouth. But somehow, strangely, only with her, only with Mary Elizabeth. Why was that?

"Why do you do that to your hair?" Maze asked the first time she walked into the room to find Mary Elizabeth holding a scorching hot comb to a hank of it.

"Well, why *don't* you do it to yours?" she might have snapped in reply, but didn't. Other girls had already tried with Maze. Dare Mills and Ferne Denney (who would be crowned May Queen at the end of that first year), blond, blue-eyed roommates two doors down from Maze and Mary Elizabeth, had cooed at her like she was a baby the first time they'd laid eyes on her.

"Oooh! Would you look at those freckles? And I wish you'd let me get my hands on those curls, Maze," Ferne squealed. "You'd have a nice head of hair if you just got them under control."

Dare looked Maze over from head to toe in a way only Dare Mills, who was from Ohio, could do, letting her gaze come to rest on Maze's faded, old-fashioned cotton blouse. "Grace," she said (she refused to call Maze by a nickname that, she said, she found peculiar), "you could be downright pretty if you tried."

Maze's answer? A toss of her curls, a quiet, breathy little laugh, and then, yes, silence. Simply staring back at Dare—a gleam in her eye, more than a hint of a challenge in that unblinking gaze. One night during their first week in Ladies Hall, Mary Elizabeth stepped out of the bathroom down the hall from their room, and there in the hallway she found Maze, cornered again by

Ferne and Dare. At first she assumed they were after her again about her hair, which she'd taken to pulling back in a big, unwieldy braid so the girls on the hall would stop grabbing at her curls. But then Mary Elizabeth heard what Ferne was saying, with Dare standing next to her and nodding her agreement.

"My daddy made sure before I came that I wouldn't have to share a room with one of them. If you just asked, I know they'd have to let you change."

Ferne's back was to Mary Elizabeth, and Maze, who stood leaning dreamily against the wall, saw her approaching well before Ferne finished and turned to see what Maze was looking at. She kept quiet, watching her roommate's slow approach. As Mary Elizabeth passed the three of them, Maze simply looked over at her and said, "Hard to sleep with all the racket some folks make, ain't it, Mary Elizabeth?" Then she shook her head, laughed a hollow little laugh, and followed her roommate into their room while Ferne and Dare stared at the floor and slunk back into theirs.

Visitor

1938 · 1943

Vista Combs, Maze's mother, had scraped knees and bruised shins long past the age when a girl ought to have stopped having such things. That was Vista's mother's one and only observation about her fifteen-year-old daughter on her final visit home to Torchlight, Kentucky, in 1938.

"What does my mama do in Memphis?" Vista had asked her grandmother once as a child, and her mamaw, a woman of few words, had simply said, "Well, I don't reckon we'd want to know." And that was the last time Vista asked.

Her mother showed up every few years for a meal and a night's sleep and to borrow money, her hair blackened and permed and her lips painted ruby-red. She was the only person who ever called Vista by her given name: "And how's the little Visitor doin'?" she'd croon on her way up the front steps, lacing her fingers through Vista's dark curls absentmindedly. Then on she'd go, in search of her own mother, and Vista would go back to playing with her rag doll or rereading one of the Elsie Dinsmore books

Miss Drury had lent her. The fact that this guest was her mother hardly seemed to register.

But her mother would laugh with Mamaw Marthie. They shared the same sense of humor, if nothing else. Years later, Vista would learn that they'd chosen her name, with a smile and a wink, together. Visitor Lane Combs—named both for the long-gone male visitor who'd left the way he had come, along the back lane, and for another visitor, the monthly kind, that failed to show up after the first one had left. Over time, and at the teacher Miss Drury's urging, Mamaw had shortened the name to Vista. But on her mother's infrequent visits, she was always reminded: "And how's the little Visitor?" And all Vista thought then, though she never said it, was, Seems to me you're the only visitor here.

When they learned her mother had been hit by a streetcar and killed, not too long after that visit when Vista was fifteen, Vista didn't shed a tear, and if Mamaw mourned, Vista never saw it.

The only real sadness in her life that long, hot summer was the fact that Miss Drury was gone. She'd finally finished her own schooling over at Berea, and she'd met and married another schoolteacher and moved north with him, to Ohio. North seemed to be where everyone was moving who could get there, for the factory jobs and houses with brand-new kitchens, a million miles away from any old Kentucky hollow and outside the grip of coal or lumber.

Even as a child, Vista had understood where the color of evil came from: coal. Evil was black like coal, which had killed her papaw before she could even know him and made her mother run away to Memphis to get away from all those wide-shouldered, blackness-breathing men. But when she got to feeling sad about it all, Vista would think about Miss Drury and her brand-new house in Ohio, her kitchen bright yellow and filled with sun, as Vista imagined it—no ragged trees or rocky hillside to block a single ray of light.

Mamaw Marthie had not objected to her going to school, as it was only the two of them at home most of the time and there wasn't much of anything left to do—just a little patch of greens to tend and a rooster and laying hen to feed. So when Miss Drury Badgett showed up with a pair of shoes that just fit the child's feet and brushed her dark curls and made a fuss about her pretty freckles, there seemed to be no reason not to let her go.

That was when Vista was eight and didn't know the first thing about the alphabet, much less what it meant to read. And it was a ragtag group, that first class at Miss Drury's Torchlight school (really just a room off to the side of the Free Light Church). Six holler children, all of them younger than Vista—no other child her age could be spared for school—and Miss Drury cleaned each one up and made sure they all had shoes for the walk. And then she started them on the alphabet. By the time Vista was twelve, the school had grown to fifteen pupils, and she was charged with helping the little ones with their letters.

And then she was happy, comforted by her importance and the ever-present softness of Miss Drury's eyes and hands. When she wasn't busy at the school, she'd wander through the hills in search of pretty spots to sit and read the latest book Miss Drury had given her—brushing through brambles that she hardly noticed, in love with the birdsongs and the sweet mountain air and the way, when she read those books, everything around her seemed to smell and sound so much more alive. That was how she kept on getting scrapes and bruises—well past the age when most girls had stopped, it was true, but she never even noticed, and she certainly didn't care.

But then Miss Drury left, when Vista was fourteen, and Vista turned moony-eyed and sad. While her black curls (always brushed now), combined with those surprising freckles and a sweet, dimpled smile and even sweeter singing voice at church, could make a boy look twice, most knew not to bother by the time Vista was a womanly sixteen and her beloved teacher was gone and her mama was dead, though she'd say she hardly noticed. Now Vista's smile rarely showed up at all.

One thing, and one thing only, could make Vista smile as she grew into womanhood, when even her beloved books were no longer enough; there was no one to talk to about them, after all. That thing was music and dancing. She never missed a church singing retreat or a barn dance, and with a mamaw who gave her leave to attend both as she pleased, she never bothered to notice any contradictions in those passions.

Boys loved to dance with her, though they couldn't say why. There was never any sense that the way she held their eyes or let them spin her meant a damned thing. With other girls at the dances, that kind of touch and motion might well be a prelude to other pleasures, but Vista's only interest was the music. And when she danced, she lost herself in it, just as she did when she sang the old ballads and the hymns. She'd sing "Amazing Grace" and "Down in the Valley" like she meant them; words and music did something to her, and the boys at the dances and at the retreats knew enough to realize that for Vista Combs, unlike other girls, what the words and music did was enough.

But then the Swedish boys arrived. They came to work in the lumber business that was growing outside Torchlight, taking the place of King Coal now that all the buried wealth their land could cough up was gone. They were the grandchildren of settlers who'd come to live and farm in the West—Church of the Brethren, someone said—but any religious zeal seemed to have worn its way out of the family by the time the two brothers, Paul and John Gustafson, and their cousin, the blond and blue-eyed Nicklaus Jansen, landed in Torchlight. They could work like mules, everyone said, and they were willing enough to do it, but they liked their whiskey, and the brothers, at least, knew they could have their pick of the local girls and did so on a regular basis. Nick was the quiet one, and surprisingly polite, though he could outdrink them all. And they all loved music and loved to dance. Nick could play the guitar like it was a fiddle or a banjo, and at dances that summer his presence added new life to the old songs.

Vista was seventeen when the Swedish boys arrived in Torchlight, and by the time she was eighteen, much to the amazement of everyone in and around Torchlight, she was pregnant with Nicklaus Jansen's child. To their amazement and, it must be said, their delight; what they felt was a mix of satisfaction over the comeuppance that they thought the quiet—and, they assumed, uppity—girl deserved and relief at knowing that this somber girl had found some pleasure at last.

He was a beautiful young man, too beautiful, she'd think later, blaming herself for succumbing to that beauty. He kept his blond hair longer than most men, and it curled like a baby's at his ears and the top of his neck. He was tall and strong but also thin and straight-backed; there was nothing thick or brutish about him. When Vista first saw him, walking toward Cecil Baker's barn at dusk on a summer night with his polished guitar in his hands, she felt something she hadn't quite known she could feel. Other boys, the local handsome ones, always called to mind her reckless mother somehow. But when she watched Nicklaus Jansen, his soft hands and the way he looked down at the ground rather than meet most people's eyes—like a shy little schoolboy, she thought, or like her—she banished any thoughts of her mother. And then he started to play.

He went off in a corner of the barn by himself, and Vista placed herself where she could see but not be seen, and when he started to strum chords and hum along—it was "All the Pretty Little Horses"—in a high, breathy voice, Vista had to hold on to the beam by her head to keep her balance.

Eventually his cousins came to pull him away to join the others—Cecil on fiddle and his boy Ray picking his clangy old banjo—and together they played fast and loud for the rest of the night. Vista joined the dancing then, but the whole time what she was hearing in her head was a sweet little lullaby in a schoolboy's voice, and every time she got near the musicians, she'd sneak a glance his way. But he was always looking down or over at his fellow players, watching what they did or watching his own beautiful fingers when he'd play the melody and the other two would pick and bow in the background and look at him, like everyone did, with admiration.

That was how it went at every barn dance at Cecil Baker's—and they had them regularly that summer, now that the Swedish boys were there. Nicklaus Jansen and his cousins would arrive at sunset, wearing clean shirts and their work boots; Paul and John would make straight for the whiskey at the back of the barn, and Nicklaus would head for a corner to warm up on his guitar. And each night Vista would find her place in the shadows to watch and listen.

One night, a month or so after the Swedish boys had arrived in Torchlight, something made her pull her face out of the darkness and into the light, right where Nicklaus Jansen could see her if he happened to look up. After he'd strummed through a chorus of a song she didn't recognize, he did. He looked right at her and smiled, and he said, "I wondered if you were ever gonna come out of that corner." And that night he put down his guitar and danced for the first time, and for the last half-dozen dances of the night, his one and only partner was Vista Combs.

A funny thing about the Combses was the way they kept on having just one baby before disaster struck. At least that was how it had been since Morris and Ivy Combs, Mamaw's daddy and mama, had left their baby Marthie with a cousin, gone to scout a piece of land to the south that Morris had heard about the summer before, and died in a flood.

"No use tryin' to leave," Mamaw Marthie had come to say after losing her parents and then her daughter in the space of half her life. Of course, it could be argued that she'd lost her husband for just the opposite reason: because he'd stayed and worked in the mines like every other man he and Marthie knew. But still, Mamaw Marthie maintained, leaving that peaceful holler in a bend of the mountains never left a body better off, as far as she could see. And Vista held on to that notion, at least for a time.

It might have been that being raised in a cabin with fifteen other children, treated like one of the family, it was true, but still short, like everyone was, on food and clothing and warmth, had taught Marthie another lesson. Because besides not making any plans to leave, she'd never cared to marry again and start another family. In the one picture she had of Papaw, the stern-faced portrait from their wedding day, Mamaw Marthie, a strong, tall woman with a long face that always looked tired and sad to Vista, towered over her husband, a wiry man with a hint of mischief at the corners of his mouth. He'd played the fiddle, Mamaw Marthie told Vista, and courted her with songs and foolish riddles that made her laugh despite herself.

And, well, yes, of course she'd loved him, she'd say when Vista pestered her, just as she'd loved her impetuous, colt-like daughter ("her daddy through and through," Marthie would say at these times). But love meant loss—you couldn't have one without the other, Mamaw Marthie said, and that was every bit as true in Memphis or New Orleans or some new factory town in Indiana or Ohio as it was in a Kentucky holler. And so for her, by the age of forty, when her joints began to ache at the first sign of cold and the climb over Harmony Ridge left her weak and winded, one lone granddaughter, it seemed, was enough.

In the flush of those early days with Nicklaus Jansen, Vista was convinced she'd be the first to make a change. They'd have lots of babies, that much she knew. They'd fix up Mamaw's cabin and add on rooms, and their babies would play outside in the sun-shine in the green valleys, and they'd learn their letters and read all the books Miss Drury had left. And their father would teach them to play guitar, and she would teach them to sing, and they'd be noisy and happy, all of them, outside dancing in the wind that blew off the ridge above the cabin. There would always be sun poking through. The hills would always be green and rich with summer, the redbud poking up out of the mist in the morning, music and love in all their golden heads.

Who could feel otherwise with a soft and golden lover like Nicklaus Jansen? He was as gentle as early morning, and the first time he kissed her and held her, she wondered how she ever could have felt, about love, the way her mama had made her feel—dirty, mistrustful, afraid. His soft curls felt like goose down against her cheek, and he told her—and she could tell he meant it—that she was the first: that he'd never met another girl as sweet and pure as she.

When they learned she was pregnant, they arranged a quiet wedding in the Red Lick Church. His cousins stood up with him, Mamaw Marthie with her; it was early autumn, and Vista wove wild asters through her dark curls. Nicklaus smiled at her when the preacher pronounced them man and wife, but his eyes looked glassy, she thought. Later, back at the cabin in their wedding bed, he closed his eyes, which still looked glassy and faraway; it seemed like he was trying to place himself somewhere else. And then— on her wedding night, of all times—it felt, for a moment, more like she'd always been afraid it would feel. A little shameful, connected with animals. But while he slept she shook that idea out of her head and watched him—his full, curving lips, his ruddy cheek, blond curls tossed around the pillow and over his forehead, and she wondered how she ever could have doubted the pure rightness of loving him.

Finally, in the wee hours of the morning, she pulled the crushed asters from between her curls and brushed her hair, then burrowed deep under the newly ticked comforter that had been Mamaw Marthie's wedding gift to them, wrapping herself around her warm, sleeping husband. When she woke several hours later, she was alone.

She walked into the kitchen to find Mamaw Marthie pulling a pan of biscuits from the stove, no sign of her new husband anywhere. Mamaw looked at her with a question in her eyes, then busied herself with turning the biscuits out to cool. Vista said nothing on her way to the door. Outside, the sunlight was brilliant white, stinging her eyes; the only thing out there were two noisy crows, pecking uselessly at the dead grass.

Not knowing what to do with herself, Vista walked out to the end of the lane, where it met up with the road into Torchlight. She even climbed over some of the trails up the ridge behind the cabin in the hope that Nicklaus Jansen might have fancied an early-morning ramble through the woods on the day after his wedding. She saw no sign of him, though, and she returned to the cabin breathless and hungry, baffled by his absence and growing more concerned.

She sat down to eat one of Mamaw Marthie's biscuits with fresh clover honey, a gift from a neighbor up the holler who kept bees. When Mamaw asked, perfectly innocently, where her husband was, Vista snapped, "I don't know—I reckon he'll be back soon" and left the table to busy herself with straightening up their room.

That was when she found his note. She had carefully folded the blue organdy dress that she'd sewn herself for her wedding, noting with a wave of fear that wherever Nick had gone, he'd taken the small bag of clothing that he'd brought to the cabin the day before. Maybe, she told herself, he'd simply gone into town to return the suit he'd rented for the wedding, and he was simply wearing the other clothes he'd brought.

With that thought, she turned to make the bed, overwhelmed as she did so by the urge to crawl under the covers and go back to sleep, hoping that when she woke again she'd discover that it had simply been a bad dream. There her sleeping husband would be, curled like a baby under her outstretched arm, his sweet breath tickling her neck.

When she shook the comforter and started to climb underneath it, though, a small piece of white paper floated slowly to the floor. As it floated, Vista's stomach tightened; somehow she knew, before she looked, what that piece of paper was going to say.

"I am sorry, but I believe it was a mistake for us to be married. Please try to forget about me." And it was signed, simply, "Nick."

For a long time, Vista held the note in her hands, staring at it blankly, uncomprehendingly. When she finally forced herself to take in the words, she began tearing furiously at the page, ripping it into tiny pieces that, later in the day, she would throw into the fire. At that moment, though, she gripped the pieces in her fist and shoved them under her pillow. As she did, she buried her face there and let the tears come.

Once again it was just she and her mamaw, but wasn't that all she'd ever really expected? The golden ones left that dark valley, that much had become clear. Some lived on in golden sunlight, in yellow kitchens with clear glass windows letting in all that light. Some, set on getting too much too fast, turned darker and sharper around the edges, rough and never quite clean. And then they died. All winter long, Vista held on to the life inside her, determined that this one would be one of the golden ones, one who got out, who stayed gold.

It was a harsh winter, unusually cold for eastern Kentucky, and clumps of gray ice had lodged themselves permanently in the cabin's various cracks and crevices by the end of January, when Vista's pregnancy had begun to show. Every few days she made the walk into town; she had begun to read again, since twice a week there was now a mobile library in Torchlight—an old Ford truck with crates of books in the back that parked outside the post office at eleven o'clock. It never stayed long; it didn't need to, since Vista and old Aunt Pearlie Dawson and the pale and silent Shade Nixon were the only ones who ever came.

Aunt Dawson smoked a pipe while she waited. One of the children of the cousins who had taken Mamaw Marthie in as a baby, she had never married; she'd gone off to work in a factory somewhere up North for a time, but when the coal took her papa, this time in one of the worst accidents in the history of the local mine, she'd come back to help raise the children that were younger than she.

"Mornin', Dawson." Vista would nod to her, trying to decide whether she looked like she'd been up all night and whether her breath smelled of spirits. She lived now in a room atop the Torch-light General Store, where, people said, she drank whiskey and read books all night.

"Mornin', Vista," she would answer. "Feelin' any better these days?"

"A heap better, yes, ma'am," Vista would say. She'd been sick as a dog not long after Nicklaus had left, and Mamaw had dis-cussed her morning sickness with various women in the holler, trying to recall some of the remedies they'd all tried in their day. What with the single-baby habits of the Combses, some of that lore had gotten lost; after consulting Aunt Dawson and others, though, she'd settled on wormwood tea and saltine crackers.

The other reader, Shade Nixon, had been another student of Miss Drury's, a year or two younger than Vista, pale and sickly and spurned by his brother and two sisters and the other children who walked in with them each day from above Harmony Creek, at the north end of the hollow. She hadn't had to help him with his letters, as he had already known how to read—had, in fact, been reading the family Bible and anything else he could get his hands on since his mother had taught him at the age of four. When she had died, when Shade was six or seven, he'd joined the other children at Miss Drury's school. Miss Drury had made such a fuss over him and the way he could already read anything put in front of him. But none of that seemed to matter to Shade. Nothing appeared to reach him at all, in fact.

Since Miss Drury had left, Vista hadn't seen much of him. He was never at services at the Red Lick Church—not that Vista was a regular attender, but when she did show up, for Christmas or Easter, say, Shade's father and three or four of his brothers and sisters might be there, but Shade would never come along. He worked for the timber company, doing the books, and he seemed to be as scorned and isolated as ever. Whenever the truck was running late and she, Shade, and Aunt Dawson stood inside the post office door to wait, Vista sometimes tried to strike up a conversation with him. But he would never meet her eye.

One morning, as she took her books to the driver to have

them listed in the record book, she stepped back to let Shade go ahead of her, claiming she'd forgotten one other book she wanted. But really she wanted a chance to see what he was taking out. That morning it was Shakespeare's *A Winter's Tale* and something by a woman whose name she didn't recognize, but he had several other items as well—small brown envelopes with labels on the outside.

"Shade, what are those other things you've got there?" she asked, and before he could answer, the driver piped in with "Well, don't you know you can get music recordings here now, too?"

"Well, no, I don't," Vista snapped back to the know-it-all college-boy driver, whom she'd never liked. And because she knew it would be a good way to get at a good Christian Berea boy's heart, she added, "Where do you suppose somebody like *me's* gonna go to play herself any records?"

Shade Nixon just cleared his throat and signed his name in the record book. As he turned to leave, though, he tipped his hat to Vista. "If you need a Victrola," he said, "I could give you mine. I've been meanin' to buy a new one next time I get in to Pikeville." And then he hurried on up the road toward the timber company's temporary office next to the feed store.

A week later, he was there with it: a big old box of a thing with a horn-shaped piece that screwed onto the side. "I reckon I can carry it on out to your place after work," he said, and this time it was Vista who couldn't think of what to say. So Shade went on, "Be sure to check out something to play on this thing, now," and he carried it back to his office.

She was nervous and flustered then, afraid to ask the know-it-all college boy about the records he had that day. But then she heard Aunt Dawson, suddenly there behind her back. "Go on, now, girl, don't be 'fraid of that boy," she said, and as she said it, Vista felt her baby give her a good, swift kick at the right side of her belly. She laughed then, grabbing hold of old Aunt Dawson's arm.

She picked out one record that morning—songs by the Carter Family, including some she recognized from dances and camp meetings: "Bury Me Under the Weeping Willow," "River Jordan," "Cannon Ball." She was afraid to take more than one record, and in truth she didn't recognize any of the other names on the labels.

Shade showed up just a few minutes after four that day, and he showed Vista and Mamaw Marthie how to wind up the Victrola and put the needle down easy, right at the first groove on the shiny black disc. Vista thought she saw him frown just a little bit when he looked at the record she'd brought home.

"You only wanted one?" he asked her, and she nodded, embarrassed to admit it was the only one she'd recognized. They gave him a good hot meal for his efforts, and though he didn't have much to say, he did look up from the floor from time to time.

After Shade left, she and Mamaw Marthie played the thing over and over. Mamaw stared endlessly at the spinning record, but Vista found that it made her dizzy to do so, and she stared out at the snow while Mother Maybelle sang. Finally, after they'd played the record perhaps a dozen times and the sun had started to drop behind the western ridge, Mamaw stood to clear the dishes from the table while Vista dozed in her chair beside the stove. The record's spinning was slowing gradually, and the needle purred along its edge, making rhythmic popping noises that sounded a little like music, too.

When Vista opened her eyes, Mamaw Marthie smiled at her. "You reckon Shade Nixon's decided to court you, little Visitor?"

Vista opened her eyes wide and looked down at her protruding stomach, and then they both burst into laughter that was as loud as the singing from the Victrola had been. Vista realized it was the kind of thing her mama would have laughed about with her mamaw. All of a sudden, the idea of a man—any man, but particularly Shade Nixon—making his way up the back lane to their cabin to court her seemed unbearably funny, the kind of funny that left you laughing till you thought you just might cry.

Pilgrim and Stranger

1961

Two girls and their big wooden boxes. Their machines. When Maze and Mary Elizabeth weren't in their room or at class or a meal, or off on a long Saturday hike, that was where you'd find them that fall: Maze at a loom, Mary Elizabeth at a piano in the Music Building. The piano teacher at Berea, Mr. Roth, was stunned by Mary Elizabeth's skill; the first time he heard her play, he told her he had nothing to teach her.

"Where'd you learn to play like that?" he asked. He didn't mean it unkindly, Mary Elizabeth knew, yet she'd heard the extra emphasis, however slight, he'd placed on the *you*. It rankled, but she would not let that show.

She looked down at her hands on her lap. "First from my aunt. She lived for some years in Paris and learned there," she said. "Then from Professor Hallis at the University of Kentucky." She looked up, knowing Mr. Roth would be waiting for further explanation. "He was a friend of hers."

"I see." The young teacher, who was probably only a few years older than Mary Elizabeth, nodded slowly, watching her. "Well," he said, "I may not have much to teach you, but I can work with you, and I can make some folks around here sit up and take notice of you." A few days later, he arranged for her to play for the College president and the board of trustees at a special concert in December. They got started on a program right away.

"Only two pieces," Mr. Roth said, a relief to Mary Elizabeth. His lanky blond hair was always falling in his eyes, and he whisked it back now with delicate fingers. "More than that and the old geezers'll start nodding off. You like the Frenchmen, so let's have you play one of the Debussy pieces. And then Chopin. You should work on the *Études*."

She agreed. Secretly she was ecstatic at the thought. Aunt Paulie, who'd loved Chopin, had worked with her on some of the *Waltzes*. "Like the sound of a steady rain when there's been a long, dusty drought" was how she'd described it after she'd played the "Waltz in E Minor" on her record player. Mr. Roth loved it when Mary Elizabeth recalled the things Aunt Paulie had said. Cortot was a nervous little collaborator. Ravel was a mama's boy. Horowitz had hands like racehorses. Gottschalk stole his best ideas from black musicians. He'd make her take a break and have some tea and tell him stories about her aunt. He'd toss back his blond hair and laugh with abandon.

There was one thing she would eventually wish she *hadn't* told him. Aunt Paulie always wished she'd been able to play Stravinsky. *Petrushka*, the version he'd adapted for piano. Three movements, and she'd never mastered any of them. That was one Mary Elizabeth should have kept to herself.

"We'll work on that, then, after the concert in December" was Mr. Roth's answer the day, after a lesson in late September, when she told him. "You'll master it, and then you'll play it at an even bigger concert at the end of the year. President, trustees, all the big-money people, all the faculty . . . it'll be marvelous. They'll see how good you are, what you can do; you'll prove it to them." He never mentioned her race. He didn't have to. What she never understood was why it seemed to matter so much to him. It unnerved her, and it made her talk too much, made her tell him too many things.

Both of them, Maze and Mary Elizabeth, were happier that fall than either had expected to be at Berea. On bright autumn Saturdays, after practicing and weaving through the morning, they'd hike into the hills together, out along Scaffold Cane or up the rocky slope of the hill they called Devil's Slide, sandwiches and water in a rucksack that they took turns carrying. Town boys in cars along Scaffold Cane—"scoads," the students called them— would yell at them out their windows. But they barely noticed, Mary Elizabeth's fingers still tingling and her ears filled with Chopin, Maze walking, unconsciously, to the rhythm of her feet on the loom that morning.

They talked on their hikes about many things. Mary Elizabeth's progress on the Études, Maze's battles with the know-it-all girl who'd replaced the former weaving crew chief.

Maze had hidden her skill at the loom to get the college work assignment she wanted: part of the crew of weavers working at the varied looms in the Weaving Cabin. There they created table runners and blankets and throws to sell at the stores in town. Technically, students assigned to the weaving crew were supposed to be novices, learning a new skill, but when her crew supervisor saw how quick and efficient a weaver Maze already was—and how quickly his crew would therefore be able to fill its quotas—he pretended not to notice that there would be little left for her to learn.

She'd learned from Sister Georgia, the woman her mother had cared for, on a big old loom that had belonged to the early Shakers. Georgia had learned at Berea, where she'd been a teacher sixty years before. Though she bickered endlessly with Maze's mother, with Maze Georgia was endlessly patient and tender, a perfect teacher. Maze was competent at the big loom at twelve, accomplished by fourteen; Vista sold the table covers she and Georgia made to the owners of the Beau Rive Hotel, where she was a laundress.

Maze never tired of it, and knowing she could weave while at Berea was one of the things that had made her give in to Vista and agree to go. Even the monotony, the rhythmic sameness—in fact, especially this—soothed her. She was known to sneak into the Weaving Cabin after hours, even sometimes to skip a class or two, to finish work on a complicated overshot blanket or one of her favorites, the pretty indigo Bronson weave.

"You'd best keep your mouth shut, you know," Mary Elizabeth warned her, "if you want to keep that job. And you'd best slow down a little and make a few mistakes." She'd watched Maze at the loom many times; often, as their dormitory's eleven o'clock curfew approached and Maze still wasn't back at the room, she had hurried over to the Weaving Cabin to drag her there.

"Don't you ever get bored with it?" Mary Elizabeth couldn't help asking one night, watching Maze use her feet to manipulate the rows of yarn, then lift and slide the shuttle, over and over again, counting, Mary Elizabeth knew, the whole time—even while she talked. Mary Elizabeth's own eyes glazed as she watched; try as she might, she could never remember which was warp and which was weft, could never understand how the whole contraption worked, how the pattern at Maze's side was transferred to this massive rack of wood and wires, sticks and strings, and rows of yarn that somehow came together into a big expanse of patterned cloth, soft and lovely, this time in muted pink and gray.

"Bored?" Maze said, still counting somewhere in her head, somehow. "Well, no. Do you get bored when you play the piano? Don't you go other places in your mind while you're playin'? Don't you forget about all the pads and wires inside the thing and just feel the music in your bones somehow? Isn't that what you told me the other night after you played?"

She'd stopped now, and she was looking at Mary Elizabeth. It was hard to read her expression.

"I didn't mean that to be insulting, Maze," Mary Elizabeth said, worried.

"I'm not insulted. I'm just sayin' that while I'm doin' this, I can go anywhere I want to in my head." She tied a thread and moved the shuttle and started up on the pedals again. "Back to Pleasant Hill." She spoke in rhythm with her moving legs. "Back up Devil's Slide. Places I have never even been." Her feet did not stop moving, her fingers somehow tracking rows even as she spoke.

Mary Elizabeth was still baffled. "But how do you not lose track?"

"Well." Beat, beat. "How can you"—beat—"pound those keys"—beat—"and talk to me the way I've seen you do?" Beat, beat.

Mary Elizabeth laughed and shook her head. "Only when I play the old hymns, girl, you know that. I can do those in my sleep."

"Well, it's like I'm doin' this in my sleep sometimes, too," Maze said, stopping again now, tying another thread. She smiled and started up again, looking at Mary Elizabeth. "Just dreamin' along." Beat. "A *pil*grim and a *stran*ger," beat, "I *jour*ney here below," she was singing now—the words to a hymn they'd sung at chapel services the week before, one that had made Maze roll her eyes and laugh.

"Far *dis*tant is my *coun*try," Mary Elizabeth joined in, singing with the same stilted emphasis to the beat Maze set with her feet. "The *home* to which I *go*."

Christian talk about heaven set Maze's teeth on edge; at chapel services, she'd scowl and slump down in the pew at any talk of a better life beyond. "What's any of that got to do with livin' right here right *now?*" she'd lean over and ask Mary Elizabeth in a stage whisper.

They finished the verse just as Maze reached the end of a row on the loom. She stopped her pedaling then, and the college bells started to chime eleven o'clock. There was really no comparison, Mary Elizabeth thought as they walked back to their room, humming together. Though truthfully, she *could* go somewhere else, the way Maze described, when she played certain things. Maybe the Debussy "Reflections in the Water" from the *Images*, the piece she'd learned first. Certainly some of the hymns, the old ones that she still loved. "Precious Lord," "I'll Fly Away," "Wayfaring Stranger," "Amazing Grace"—Maze's hymn.

But it was all changing now, her playing. It started when Mr. Roth had arranged for her to play for the college president and his wife and some of their guests at a reception at the beginning of October. She'd played pieces she knew well, really in the background, while they all drank their punch and talked, but eventually the front parlor of the president's house, with its beautiful grand piano, had grown quiet and everyone had stopped to listen, looking over at her. She'd nearly forgotten where she was, but she'd closed her eyes and recovered and kept on playing.

When she'd first arrived at the house, she'd been told to go around back, to the kitchen, where the other servers were. Until the president's wife had seen her and stepped over to invite her in. "You must be the pianist we've been hearing so much about!" she said. And Mary Elizabeth knew why they'd been hearing about her, why the president's wife knew immediately who she was, but she smiled, then looked down at the ground and said, "Yes, ma'am, I've come to play."

Now every week or so someone from the president's office called Mr. Roth to schedule something else. An alumni dinner. The opening of a new building. They'd started trotting her out for every donor or newspaper reporter they could get on campus. Hers was "the new face of Berea College." Over the Thanksgiving recess, Mr. Roth told her, he'd be heading up to Louisville to pick up the sheet music for *Petrushka* that he'd ordered.

But hers wasn't the face of Berea College. Not even the "new" face. Not her real face, anyway, the face none of those white men in suits and women in pearls ever saw, the face no one ever saw. Except maybe Maze, sometimes.

Maze, who didn't care at all about whom Mary Elizabeth played for the rest of the time, really only wanted her roommate to play private concerts for her, any night she could get her to, over at the lounge where she'd played that second night they were together. After dinner, after their work assignments, after studying, whenever she wasn't weaving, whenever she could get Mary Elizabeth to go.

When Maze wasn't weaving, she always seemed to have the time. Maze would cut class, miss curfew, spend all kinds of extra hours at the Weaving Cabin just because she liked it more than studying. Mary Elizabeth's work assignment, on the other hand, was washing dishes after meals in the cafeteria, along with most of the other black students that year. That was the only other time she could let down her guard, show her true face. For twelve hours a week.

Her daddy told her, the night before she left, never to slip. He needn't have said anything; by then she was already expert at it. Live where they live, eat where they eat, learn where they learn—but keep your eyes down. Do it all well, but not so well they think you're uppity. Let them know you aren't a threat.

Aunt Paulie would have laughed at that advice, then spat on the ground. But that was why her daddy did his best to limit her aunt's influence. Mary Elizabeth had figured that much out early. Once a week for her lesson when she was younger, an occasional overnight for a concert in Lexington after that. But with explicit instructions then: no jazz. No exposure to the men and women who might normally play music at Aunt Paulie's house on a Saturday night.

And one unforgettable time, for a trip to Cincinnati to hear a young pianist Aunt Paulie had heard about, playing with the symphony at Music Hall. Mary Elizabeth was twelve then. "I want to do that," she said to Aunt Paulie when the lights came up at the end. It was the only time Aunt Paulie, whose eyes were wet with tears, couldn't answer her. She only looked away.

By the time Mary Elizabeth was eighteen and ready for college, she knew the drill. Funny that now, at Berea, the only times she could show her real face, and rest, were when she was sleeping and when she was working. There in the bowels of the kitchen, with other students like her, who were every bit as tired as she was. You could see it in their faces while they scraped and scrubbed, rinsed and dried.

And sometimes, too, with Maze. She realized this on a bright, cold day early in November when they climbed Devil's Slide. They'd stopped for water and to talk a bit. Usually on their walks, their talk eventually came around to some version of Maze's main preoccupation: Who are our mamas, and will we become like them?

Maze generally did most of the talking. Vista distrusted most men, she said. Maze didn't know enough to decide whether to trust them or not. Vista was ashamed to have come from the mountains of eastern Kentucky; Maze would move there, to her Mamaw Marthie's crumbling old cabin, in a heartbeat if she could. And she'd take Sister Georgia and the big old loom in the Sisters' Shop with her.

Vista was a Baptist, though not a very devout one. Maze didn't necessarily believe in God, though she had some sense of a spirit, or spirits, and she had believed Sister Georgia and the other old Shakers when they'd said they saw them. In fact, Maze said, she sometimes thought of becoming a Shaker herself, even though the only other one left in the state of Kentucky, or west of the Appalachian Trail, for that matter, was Sister Georgia.

On this November Saturday, though, Maze was pensive. Mary Elizabeth was even quieter. Her practicing had not gone well that morning. The day before, she'd gotten a letter from her father; her mother was back in the hospital, he said.

Maze took a long drink of water and looked over at Mary Elizabeth. They were sitting on a wide rock. The trees had shed many of their leaves, and the air was crystal-clear. Below them they could see bits of the town and campus through the normally dense curtain of leaves, the spire of a church here and there, smoke from a handful of chimneys.

"You know, M. E.," Maze said (she'd begun to call her that, finding that nothing else, like the shorter Mary or Mary Liz, seemed to suit her, she said), "I believe you're right. Your eyes *do* look as sad as your mama's sometimes. Maybe even sadder. Why is it you never tell me any news about her and your daddy?" And Mary Elizabeth began to cry.

She started talking then, inexplicably telling Maze things, too many things. Her mother was sick or something, she said, not quite right in the head.

"Not right in the head?" Maze said, and the words sounded horrible, echoing back to Mary Elizabeth like that. "What does that mean?"

Of course Maze would never do the delicate, tactful thing. Change the subject, look away. Not Maze. Maze would thunder onward, ask for more.

All right, then, Mary Elizabeth decided. All right, then.

Sometimes her mother had fits of a sort, and they'd have to steer her up to her room and put her to bed. Once they did, she might not emerge for days.

Fits? What kind of fits?

Talking to herself. Almost like she was singing. But in a

language no one could understand. *Ah bay. Rorororo. Thissss, tisss, sisss.* Strange like that. Nonsense. Quiet-like usually, but still, of course people would stare.

What kind of singing? Like a hymn? Pretty like that? Or sad sometimes like when you play the piano? Maybe she wanted to sing along.

No, no—not like that. How to convey that terrifying sound? It *could* have been music almost, sometimes, like a kind of singing, maybe like blues singing. Low and kind of rumbling, scary almost. In a minor key if it was in any key at all. Just a few strange sounds, and she'd repeat them over and over.

"I went to a prayer service over in Torchlight once when I was little," Maze said, "over in the mountains, and when the people there got the spirit, that's what they sounded like. Kind of like animal sounds, growls and mumbles, but it also sounded like words some of the time, just words in a language I didn't know. Then they'd fall on the ground and jerk around, and when it was all over they went right back to being normal, singin' hymns and actin' just like everyone else."

"I suppose they handled snakes, too."

"M. E., I'm just sayin'—"

"I know what you're sayin', Maze, but my daddy doesn't believe in all that getting the spirit and speaking in tongues nonsense. That's not part of his church, and it wasn't part of my mama's growing up, either, and that is not what she is doing when this happens to her."

"Well, who said anything about your daddy's church? I

thought we were talkin' about your mama, about her not be-ing right in the head, in your words! Isn't that what you just—"

"She has tried to kill herself. For all I know, she's just tried again. My daddy says she's in the hospital, and he didn't say why. But I can guess. He says I can't visit her till I come home for Christmas break and she's out of the hospital again. He says it's her 'woman troubles.' But that's what he's always told me."

She was weeping now—big, fat tears, snot running from her nose. Maze tried to reach for her, but she pulled away and got up from the rock.

God, she thought. Not right in the head? Whose words were those? But how else could she say it?

Maze was talking again, she would never stop talking, but it came out a whisper now. "You reckon she was tryin' to make those fits go away when she tried to kill herself?"

Mary Elizabeth felt exhausted suddenly, afraid she might not make it back down the trail. She looked over at the build-ings she could see, the late-afternoon sun hitting the roofs and making them gleam. "I don't know, Maze," she said, wiping her wet eyes and face with the back of her hand. "I'm tired. Let's go back."

"All right, M. E.," Maze said, but she didn't move from the rock.

Mary Elizabeth started down the trail on her own, and be-fore she'd gone far she heard Maze behind her. She felt a hand on her shoulder, and when she turned around, Maze was there with a handkerchief. She wiped Mary Elizabeth's eyes and cheeks tenderly, then smoothed her hair away from her face and behind her ears.

"I imagine there's more goin' on with your mama than 'woman troubles,' whatever that is," she said. "Probably more than you'll ever know. I don't know why they think they can't tell us who they are, but it seems like that must be what they think." She put the handkerchief in Mary Elizabeth's hand.

Mary Elizabeth nodded, not really hearing. When they got back to campus, they went straight to the cafeteria for supper, and Mary Elizabeth was glad to stay on after to work, washing piles of dishes in a fog of exhaustion. She was glad to be away from Maze and all her questions, all her theories. Glad just not to think about it anymore.

M ary Elizabeth wouldn't go with her because, she said, while she did like the old hymns, she didn't have much use for hillbilly music—the term everyone seemed to use for the music Maze had learned to love as a child. Some of Maze's earliest memories were of Vista playing songs like "Cripple Creek" and "Single Girl, Married Girl" on an old wind-up Victrola in her Mamaw Marthie's cabin.

She certainly wasn't going to ask any of the other girls on their hall, so Maze went to her first Berea Country Dancers square dance in the school gymnasium on her own, on the Saturday night before Thanksgiving. It wasn't just the music, she knew. Mary Elizabeth had seemed far away from Maze since the day she'd talked about her mama. She claimed it was because she was so busy, because she needed to practice every minute she wasn't studying or working, to get ready for her recital in a few weeks. But Maze felt like Mary Elizabeth was avoiding her, and she found it hurtful. And that made her restless.

Even weaving didn't help. She felt fidgety, itching for something to happen, forced indoors by the cold and damp of late fall. She'd seen posters for the Saturday-night dances and longed to go, but she feared she'd be lost without a partner. At home you needed a partner for the barn dances she'd gone to outside Harrodsburg, and she always went with her sometimes boyfriend Darrell. Since coming to Berea, those were the only times she'd really missed Darrell: Saturday nights, when she felt like dancing.

Finally, on that unusually warm November night, Maze decided just to walk to the school gymnasium on her own. And that was how she met Harris Whitman.

She watched him dancing for a while at first. It wasn't the first time she'd seen him. He was tall and thin, with curly dark hair and a neatly trimmed beard; he lived in town, and Fern and Dare and some of the other girls on Maze and Mary Elizabeth's hall, who found him handsome and mysterious, had learned all they could about him. He wasn't a student at Berea, though he had been a year or two before; he'd stayed on in town, working as a woodworker, selling the furniture he made through a couple of the local stores. He was also a rabble-rouser, the owner of one of the stores had told Fern. Involved with unions and the like, noisy about state politics. Because he was so handsome, that kind of activity only added to his allure. Had he been a different man, homely or even just regular-looking, interests like those would have made him a pariah in those girls' eyes, Maze knew.

He wasn't married, they reported, though he did go out from time to time with Miss Perrin, the new art teacher at Berea, who was from Pennsylvania and, the girls claimed, looked down her nose at everyone else in town. Except Harris Whitman, apparently.

Maze found their interest in him ridiculous, and she told them so. He was nice enough to look at, yes, but they didn't know one meaningful thing about him, she said, only further confirming their sense of Maze's peculiarity, with her funny name and her wild gold hair that she refused to straighten or tease. Not to mention the way she spent all her time at her work assignment or with her roommate, that colored girl.

"Well, like you said, M. E., I am one odd girl," Maze would say when the two of them walked by a cluster of blond Berea girls and heard them snicker. Somewhere along the line, Maze had stopped caring about the fact that those girls felt that way. By now, she knew that Mary Elizabeth didn't find her all that strange. Or maybe she still did, but she didn't care. When Maze reminded her of the night she'd called her "odd," Mary Elizabeth only laughed and rolled her eyes, nodding at the memory of her first response to Maze.

Maze hadn't cared one way or another about Harris Whitman before that night, when she walked into the gym to the sound of the musicians playing "Sally Goodin" and saw him dancing. Even with a fast tune like that, there was a softness in the way he moved, and an effortlessness; he'd guide his partner with the gentlest touch at the small of her back as they promenaded down a row, then spin her and catch her up, his long fingers at her waist.

He danced with a number of different partners, and Maze saw no sign of Miss Perrin, who probably didn't care for hillbilly music, either, Maze supposed. From the first dance she watched, Maze knew she had to dance with him, had to feel that hand on her back, her arm, her waist. When Dr. Wendt, her philosophy professor, saw her and walked over to ask her to dance with him when they called the next reel, she was happy enough to walk out with him. But the whole time she kept one eye on Harris Whitman, who was sitting that one out, standing and talking by a table near the back of the gym and drinking a Coke.

"Nice that you came, Miss Jansen," Dr. Wendt was saying to her across the row as they waited their turn. "Not many students come out for the country dances."

Maze looked around the gym and realized it was true; most of the other dancers were older or else much younger, kids, really, probably the children of some of the older dancers. Still another thing to make her odd, Maze thought, imagining Fern and Dare's reaction to seeing her dance with Dr. Wendt. But so be it. She loved a good country dance. She hadn't realized how much she had missed it.

Dr. Wendt was a pleasant if rather wooden dancer, which somehow didn't surprise her. Before the reel quite ended, she curtsied in his direction and thanked him, claiming to need a bottle of pop. Before she got to the tables in the back, there was Harris Whitman, walking right toward her, back to the dance floor.

He smiled at her like he knew her, and she felt a funny kind of shiver from her stomach up to her chest. Before she had time to think about it, she said to him, "I was wondering if you'd mind dancin' one with me."

He smiled again, a different way somehow. Maybe a little sly, she thought, then sweet. How many different kinds of smiles could a man have? And then he said, "I don't believe I'd mind at all," and he reached for her hand and led her out to the middle of the floor.

But what in God's name had she done? she suddenly thought as the music reached her ears and struck her heart cold. This was a waltz! Then "Oh, I'm sorry," she mumbled, letting go of his hand. "I don't know how to dance a waltz."

He took her hand again and pulled her close, whispering as he placed his other hand on her back, just where she'd longed to have him put it, at that sweet, warm place below her waist where the heat rose up from below.

"Just relax and follow me," he said. And she let her arms and legs go soft, almost limp, leaning into him, into his own heat and the way he smelled, like the woods after a spring rain. And she did relax and follow him. She let him lead. Through that song, and through all the rest of them that evening.

Until that night, her only partners had been country boys, barn-dance stompers. At other dances, at her high school, she'd backed away from slow dances, even with Darrell, who only saw a slow dance as a chance to sneak both hands onto her behind and try to kiss her neck.

It didn't help that she was almost always taller than the boys in high school, Darrell included. Why, she often wondered, couldn't she have been raven-haired and dimpled and small as a bird, like her mother? Apparently she favored her father, a man she'd never seen. "You got the Swedish half, I reckon," Vista had told her once. "They grow them big and blond, like you."

But Harris Whitman was a good three inches taller than Maze, who was five foot nine in the flats she wore that night. She'd never known what it felt like to fit together with a man like that.

She'd worn her best dress, even though it wasn't the season for it—a lilac-colored organdy that had once belonged to another of Vista's employers, Nora Taylor, who'd been tall and thin and broad-shouldered like Maze. It had a fitted bodice and a pretty scooped neck, and Maze had always loved the way the thin, silky layers of its skirt moved against her thighs as she danced. Lucky—maybe even a little strange, she thought—that it was such a warm night for November.

That night, dancing with Harris, the soft touch of those layers, and then his leg between hers as he turned her, pressing her back with his palm and cupped fingers, was almost too much; at times, when they waltzed, she nearly cried out from the pleasure of it all. He seemed to know when she was feeling this way, and to pull her closer then. She could feel his lips on her hair, which was loose and falling in wild curls down her back.

They made a striking pair, she knew, two willowy dancers, even during the fast reels. Maze could feel the appreciative eyes of the other dancers, watching as they moved together. Harris wore black trousers and a starched white shirt that was open at the neck, and he never took his eyes off Maze. No one dared to cut in and ask her to dance, and none of the women she'd watched him dance with earlier came looking for him. Apparently, Maze thought at some point, during the last slow waltz of the night, nearly bursting with happiness, it had been just fine for her to come to one of the Berea Country Dances alone.

Mary Elizabeth didn't notice how late it was when Maze got back to the room that night. Her concert was scheduled for the following week, on Wednesday, the last day of the term. She had practiced until ten o'clock that night, then returned to their empty room. Probably Maze had gone from the dance to the Weaving Cabin, she thought as she collapsed on her bed, still in her clothes.

The next morning, Maze was sound asleep in her bed, snoring lightly, her organdy dress draped over a chair. She must have pulled the covers up over her and turned off her lamp, Mary Elizabeth realized when she was fully awake. She dressed for church in the dim morning light and tried to decide whether to wake her roommate. Maze had missed many church and midweek chapel services by now, and this didn't go unnoticed at Berea. And her grades were none too stellar, either, with all the classes she'd missed and the little studying she'd managed to do.

But then, Mary Elizabeth thought, her own grades were slipping, too, what with all the time she was spending at the piano. Why she was doing it she couldn't exactly say. Mr. Roth was pushing her, certainly, but there was something else, too, some ineffable thing. Some sort of longing, some sense of possibilities she hadn't thought of before. These days when she finished playing the "Étude," (polished now beyond her wildest imagining when she'd begun working on it last September) and closed her eyes, she saw the fingers of that pianist she'd seen as a child at Music Hall in Cincinnati. She imagined Vladimir Horowitz's fingers—like the legs of a racehorse. That strong, that rapid. When she opened her eyes and looked at her own long, slim fingers, she saw something else, though. What, exactly? Who or what was she becoming? How could she imagine herself in this way?

These days her fingers alternately ached and tingled, all day long. Mr. Roth had long ago petitioned for a change in her work assignment when he'd seen what all that dishwashing was doing to her hands. Now she cataloged books in the back rooms of the library. She was still hidden but less able to relax, with all the librarians bustling around, watching her.

For the concert, she would play on the grand piano in the alumni lounge, the same piano she and Maze had stumbled on their second night on campus, in a room with portraits of past presidents and board chairmen hung on the walls. (How had they managed not to notice these? How had they felt free to settle in there that evening?) When she thought of the upcoming concert, now less than a week away, she felt a team of horses racing through her gut. But no racehorse fingers. Unless the legs of horses ached and tingled the way her fingers did now.

She decided to let Maze sleep. One more missed church service could hardly make a difference. Closing their door quietly and walking down the hall with the other girls, all of them dressed for church, all sleepy and quiet, she wondered idly, in the back of her mind, if those could have been actual grass stains she'd seen on the back of Maze's discarded dress.

Maze longed to tell Mary Elizabeth. She imagined when, and how, to say it; she practiced. A knock on the door of the practice room in the Music Building, maybe, and then "I have fallen in love!" Or she might take her a sandwich. When, in God's name, was the girl *eating*? It seemed that all Maze saw her roommate do was sleep. And Mary Elizabeth did precious little sleeping, too. When she did, she was restless, fitful, grinding her teeth.

So a knock on the door of the practice room, and then a sandwich. Then, casually, "Remember how I decided to go to that dance last Saturday on my own?" Or "You know that fellow Harris Whitman all the girls talk about? Well, guess who he kissed. And, well, did more than that with."

But she couldn't. She couldn't tell Mary Elizabeth what she had done with him. Though she was nearly bursting with it, with the joy of it, the feel of him, his skin, his mouth. Him inside her!

Lord! The mystery of that, the complete mystery, and the surprise of it. The way she couldn't *not* find out what that would be like. "We should stop," he'd said; "I'll walk you back." And "No!" she'd tried to shout, though her voice had come out like a sob, like she was almost choking, and she'd pulled him back to her and said, "No!" again. "Please, no." She couldn't stop, couldn't let him stop, she wanted that night to go on forever, wanted his hands on her forever, would have swallowed him whole if she could have.

They were on a hill behind the gymnasium, above a little patch of woods. Far too late for a harvest moon like that night's, for the strangely warm air. Like Indian summer, but it was nearly Thanksgiving. All of it seemed not quite real. Like she was dreaming, and she couldn't let it end.

He kissed her again, and she pulled him toward her, on top of her, she pressed herself against him and felt him there, hard—so different from feeling Darrell hard against her, when she'd only wanted to pull away. Now she arched her back and pulled him tighter. He kissed her neck, he lifted up her skirt and pulled down her panties and touched her there, and it was agony while he did but more agony if he stopped, and she let herself moan and call out his name in a voice she didn't recognize.

"Where have you come from?" he asked her, panting.

From a land of fairies, she might have said. I do not remember, she might have said, right now I cannot recall. What she did say, as she reached to unbutton his trousers, was "From deep in a mountain holler."

Of course, she knew, there was no way to tell Mary Elizabeth any of this.

The concert was fine. Hadn't it been fine? Everyone said so. Everyone was smiling afterward, drinking their punch and nibbling on cookies and smiling at her—the president and his wife, three members of the board and their wives. Her father stood in a corner and beamed, one eye always on her mother, held together somehow, maybe with glue. But not smiling. Maze was there, too, with someone she didn't know—tall, bearded; who was he? Mr. Roth floating around the room, making introductions, also beaming, constantly pointing at her, smiling over at her, nodding. Saying something about her that she couldn't understand, couldn't hear, for some reason.

She couldn't hear what any of them were saying. Were they speaking to her, or about her? There were sounds, muffled sounds, getting through somehow, but when she lifted her hands after the final chord she had somehow stopped being able to hear. She had played not with her ears or her mind but with her body, as Aunt Paulie had taught her; by that evening, the Chopin "Étude," like the "Image," was a physical memory for her. Girl and machine, together, one. She was exhausted now. That had to be it. She believed she had played well. Everyone was smiling, saying she had.

Then her father looked at her across the room, and she knew it was time to walk with him and her mother to their car. She said good-bye to Mr. Roth. "Practice, practice! And Merry Christmas!"

She nodded; she had read his lips. Her bag was already packed and in the trunk of her father's car.

Then, as they walked to the parking lot, a voice behind her, one she heard this time—Maze calling out to her.

"M. E.!"

She turned. Maze was hurrying toward them, her father getting her mother into the car quickly, closing her door, hurrying around to open his own. Maze had the tall man with her still; he walked fast to keep up with her.

"Mary Elizabeth, Reverend Cox," she said. Her eyes were sparkling. She was out of breath. "This is Harris Whitman. I wanted you to meet him."

He held out his hand. Mary Elizabeth could see her father at her side, slowly closing his own door, nodding nervously, smiling. "How d'you do," he said, and shook the man's hand, then looked at his daughter.

She shook Harris Whitman's hand next. "Pleased to meet you," she said. Who are you? she thought.

"That was beautiful," he said. He still held on to her hand.

Her father cleared his throat. "We should get going, Mary Elizabeth," he said. "Your mother's tired."

The air was growing thick again, everyone's voice weirdly muted, the cotton back in Mary Elizabeth's ears. She pulled her hand back and opened the car's back door.

"I didn't get to say hello to your mama," Maze said as Mary Elizabeth climbed in. "M. E.?" She put her head in next to Mary Elizabeth's. "Couldn't I just—"

Then Mary Elizabeth pushed Maze, gently, back out of the car. Quickly, so no one else might have seen, she thought. Hoped. "Not now, Maze," she said as she did it. She tried to smile, like it was a kind of joke. But it hurt to smile, she realized; she was so tired of smiling. "I'll call you soon, Maze. We have to go now."

The engine of their old Ford roared as her daddy started it, and Mary Elizabeth rolled down her window. Maze was frowning at her, the gleam in her eyes gone. Mary Elizabeth waved, trying to make it light and funny, trying to make it better. Gotta go! Maybe another concert! My public awaits me! But she didn't say any of it.

"I'm sorry, Maze," she said, waving, as her father put the car in gear.

Then Maze reached for her hand. "I was thinkin' I might come visit you over the vacation," she yelled through the window, over the engine's noise. She looked toward the front seat. "Reverend Cox, Miz Cox, would that be all right with you?"

Mary Elizabeth watched her daddy look back at Maze and try to smile. He licked his lips and coughed, then waved as if he hadn't heard her. His wife had sunk deep into her seat, had made herself impossibly small somehow. Was she even there? Mary Elizabeth wondered.

They had to go, she knew, so she began rolling up the window. "I'll call you, Maze, okay?" she said again. "After Christmas. I promise I'll give you a call."

"But M. E., you know I don't . . ." was all she heard before she closed the window completely and her father pulled away.

Have a telephone. She doesn't have a telephone, Mary Elizabeth remembered then. But she couldn't bring herself even to turn around and wave out the rear window one more time.

Because already it had started up in the front seat. *Ah bay. Esss, sisss. Isss. Ah bay, oh.*

Mary Elizabeth wished for a long, hard rain to drown out the sound. For that cotton in her head, her ears, again. She stared at her fingers as her daddy reached for her mama's hand, trying to soothe her. She tried not to notice her mother pulling her hand away and turning to stare out her own window. *Esss. Isss. Ah bay, oh.*

Mary Elizabeth closed her eyes. She was asleep before they'd even left the campus. She didn't remember walking into her house and getting into her bed when she woke up a day and a half later, on Christmas Eve.

Sarah

1935

When she was a child, Mary Elizabeth's mother, Sarah Henry, loved the shade of the pawpaw tree, a cool drink from the running stream. She was slight and quiet, and other children from up and down the road thought her standoffish, she knew. Until she lost her older brother, Robert, and everyone said of course she turned strange. But Sarah had always been strange, and so had he, and she knew she would one day have to join him.

They said Aunt Paulie brought the music, up from the islands and all the way to Paris, then back to their little Kentucky road, to the row of shacks where she had been born. Her lover from the West Indies, his hands scarred from slips of a scythe when she met him in Louisville after the war, had left her in a cold, dirty Paris room, penniless and pregnant. Friends helped her stow away on a boat bound for New Orleans, and she must have vomited enough on that slow passage to vomit out whatever there was of a baby inside there. That spring when Sarah was eight, Aunt Paulie blew in and out of their row of sharecroppers' houses outside Stanford, Kentucky, like a breath of French perfume; she bought her ticket back to Paris with a roll of Sarah's daddy's hard-earned money—her mama never let anyone forget that. And in her wake she left the music, the start of all the trouble, people said.

But Robert had had his guitar for a year already before Aunt Paulie had landed on their doorstep. Sarah had seen him carry it out in the evenings since he was twelve. Her father had helped him string the thing. No one had to bring the music to them. It was already there.

But already, at eight, nine, ten, she was like her mother: alarmed by it. And hadn't her mother been right? This would be Sarah's husband's view eventually. Don't ask questions. Don't play that music. Avoid that kind of trouble, no matter what.

She had been frightened, too, by the smooth muscles appearing along Robert's arms, the way the sleeves of his shirt pulled tight on his arms that summer after Aunt Paulie left and Robert started walking out in the evenings with his guitar.

"Y'all and your music," her mother would say, sighing and rolling her eyes, and her voice might have been laughing, but her eyes weren't. Sarah saw that.

"Aw, let him go, girl," her daddy would say. He saw her eyes, too.

Her mother might click her tongue, but then she'd go back to taking down the wash or rinsing a bucket of poke. And down Robert would step, barely making a sound, off the porch and on down the road, never looking back, the sun setting around him, his guitar in one hand.

He was not tall, but to Sarah, lying on the porch and watching him through squinted eyes one summer evening as he left, he grew as large as the setting sun. He'd come back from a day of cutting and baling hay, his eyes red, his arms pocked with scratches and bumps. He washed and changed and put something on his hair that made it gleam like the scrubbed skin of his face. He smiled at her and reached down to pull at her hair. When he stood up and turned to go, the wideness of his back was so sudden and unexpected, it made her suck in her breath. Something stirred inside her, and she felt her mama's fear. She was ten, and he was sixteen.

She remembered because she slept on the porch that night, waiting for him. He didn't come home until dawn.

She never heard him play. How could that be? But he never played at home; her mother saw to that.

"You can play here at home when you learn to sing songs about Jesus." Then their father started to say something, but she gave him a look that suggested something more, and he lit his pipe and left for the porch.

When Sarah was a baby, they said, there was something wrong. She didn't walk until late, and then not quite right, with a slow, funny gait. She grew older but stayed small. At the creek, by herself, she could watch the little minnows for hours, dreaming of being able to move like that, to dart from place to place that suddenly, nothing hindering her.

But other children liked the creek, too, for wading and splashing, chasing crawdads. "Why you walk so funny?" a boy said one day and then pushed her down on the damp leaves and mud of the creekbed.

Instantly Robert was there, yanking the boy up by a loop of his too-short pants. "Leave her be." And after that the children did leave her alone, though they watched her like you might watch a circus freak. She'd seen pictures from the circus at school; what interested her was the look on the faces of the people in the audience. Curious and a little scared. She grew used to people watching her that way.

Reading came easily to her, and she did well at school, another thing that made her strange. She felt happy at school until Robert stopped coming, a few months after she began, as if now that he'd eased the way for her, he could be done with the thing.

"Your brother's a rounder," an older girl said to Sarah a few years later, when she was nearly twelve. The sound of the girl's breath and the shine in her eyes when she said it made Sarah feel her mama's fear again. She thought but didn't say, I bet you don't even know what that word means. She'd seen how older girls watched her brother and admired his ready smile, his slow, dreamy walk.

Sarah walked with a limp and didn't grow to look or talk like other girls her age. She kept to herself. But despite what other children or their parents, up and down the dirt road, might have said, she was not all that strange. Not yet. She didn't grow strange until Robert died.

"Your brother's a rounder."

He played the blues, they said, sometimes as far away as Lexington. But he'd come home by dawn and sleep a few hours, then work a full day alongside their father.

It was something to do with the music, then, and also the tall, smooth-muscled, near man he'd grown into. Perfect smile, a little shy, lighting up his fine-featured face.

"White girls go to those gin joints just to make their boyfriends jealous." That same older girl at school again, another time. "Your brother better watch hisself."

Black Pool Road, where they lived, ended at the creek. The last stretch ran alongside some farm fields and then a patch of woods. A few big old trees right alongside the road. She would walk there early on a Saturday morning, before the other children arrived, to listen to the quiet, watch the minnows, sit below the pawpaw tree. Maybe she was too old to be doing this, still, that spring when she was twelve. Dogwoods about to flower. Crows crowding out the sweeter-sounding birds already, only a little past dawn. Maybe if she hadn't been so small and quiet, in truth maybe already a little strange, she wouldn't have been walking to the creek when the sun was barely up, on a Saturday morning. And maybe then someone else might have found what was left of her brother, Robert, hanging from a rope tied to the biggest branch of a budding maple tree.

What in the world's hangin' there? That was her only thought. The only thing she ever remembered thinking. Still a source of shame. What in the world's growin' from that big old maple tree?

And then Aunt Paulie was back again, there to stay this time, she said. "I'm gonna take care of you," she whispered, but Sarah assumed she was talking to someone else, as she felt that she herself was already dead, already on her way to be with Robert.

Paulie handed her a notebook. "You can write in here, child," she said. "Write about anything you want. Or draw pictures. Anything. Anything at all is fine."

She looked down at the thing, barely bigger than her hand, bound with thin brown leather, then set it down on the table. Maybe, she thought, they were giving her this notebook because she'd refused to go back to school.

She also was no longer speaking. She had tried, but when she opened her mouth, after that morning, nothing emerged but a faint trickle of air. It happened when she found him. She opened her mouth to scream, but instead she gagged. Her voice flew from her. She assumed he'd taken it with him.

Other children crossed the road when she approached, as they had before. But now their eyes were cast down instead of shining with laughter. Everyone whispered around her, touched her like she was a china doll. Except Aunt Paulie, who was angry. Sometimes, Sarah thought, at her.

"Just let her be," she'd hiss when Sarah's daddy tried to get her to talk.

"You're gonna forget *how*, girl," he'd say in the evenings, pulling her onto his lap. She was still small for her age through those years, at twelve, thirteen, fourteen, and she fit comfortably there.

She wanted to please him, but she couldn't. Instead of talking, she buried her face in his sweet-smelling neck.

Before long, Aunt Paulie, who'd returned from Paris this time with a mysterious roll of money of her own, one far larger than Sarah's daddy had ever had, bought a house on Jefferson Street over in Lexington. With some more of that seemingly endless of roll of bills, she put lace curtains in the windows and a piano in the front parlor.

"How you reckon she came by all that money?" Sarah's mama asked when they went to visit her that first Sunday and Paulie stepped out of the front parlor to go make a pitcher of lemonade. "She never married, so where she's gettin' any so-called in-her-i-tance?" Her daddy only looked away and stared out the window at the quiet, shaded street. By now even Sarah knew this wasn't a question meant to be answered.

But they kept going to Aunt Paulie's house, taking the bus on Sundays after church. She played the piano for them—a lustrous sound, like water rushing, then trickling.

"No honky-tonk music, none of that in that child's ears," her mother insisted, as if Sarah wasn't standing there in the same room. It was as if they thought she'd stopped hearing as well as speaking. "We've seen clear enough what comes of that."

So on Sundays Aunt Paulie played what she called "the classics"—Chopin, Ravel, the music she'd learned to play in Paris. Claude, she said, had known musicians of every kind; he'd tuned and repaired their instruments for a living. On other days of the week, her parlor filled with musicians who lived in Louisville, and they played late into the night. Other music then—jazz, blues. Honky-tonk music. Some Fridays her father rode over to Aunt Paulie's with his friend Carl. He'd sneak home as day was breaking Saturday, smelling of whiskey and cigarettes, and for several days both he and Sarah would have to endure her mother's angry, tight-lipped silence.

But her mother needn't have worried about Aunt Paulie's influence, even when Sarah started spending occasional weekends at her house. The truth was, Sarah was afraid of her. Everything about Aunt Paulie was too large. Too large, too loud, too full of something dangerous. Like a mountain, like the giant, menacing bridge over the Kentucky River they had to cross to get to her house. Sarah had to close her eyes for that part of the trip, waiting for the crossing to end. That bridge was too high, the water of the river too far away.

Paulie *was* a large woman—tall and broad-shouldered, with a long neck and a broad forehead. Her mouth was wide and always moving—talking, smiling, smirking, laughing—her voice throaty and deep. Sarah loved the music, all of it—including, eventually, the honky-tonk tunes that wafted up to her bedroom when she stayed for a weekend. As she listened, she could almost forget her fear. But if she revealed her pleasure, the fear returned. They'd all look at her so eagerly! As if she was about to bring them news from Robert. That was all that would make it better after all, she knew. But she had no news to bring them. Her throat was dry, its passage empty. When Aunt Paulie finished playing, turned on the piano stool, and set her relentless gaze on her, Sarah only wanted to flee.

"One day you're gonna talk to me, child," she'd say in a harsh whisper. "One day you're gonna tell me all of it." And Sarah would back away, looking down at the floor but nodding, too—nodding just to get her aunt to turn her ruthless gaze on someone, or something, else.

What no one seemed to understand was that so far Robert had sent no messages. And as for what she had seen that day: There were no words for that. And what she'd seen was all there was, all there would be, for her, forevermore.

Alone at night in the loft where she slept, her parents still rustling below, she would try out whispered sounds for a new way to speak, to say it. A new language with room for what she knew.

Ahhh. Bay. Ah bay. Ah bay been.

See seen sin. Seen sin ah.

Bay, ah bay, oh.

Seen. Ssss. Sssst. Sttt.

I been, I seen.

Seen, ssst. Step stop sttt.

Row row row. Light like thissss. Sssss.

Ah bay. Oh. Stt. Stttst.

This was how she could bear, at least, to close her eyes and go to sleep. By repeating the sounds of a different language. Words for what no one else in the living world knew.

Three years after Robert's death, when she did finally decide to speak again, to use their words, their useless sounds, it wasn't

Aunt Paulie who persuaded her. It was George Cox, eighteen years old to her fifteen, back from his first year at the Lincoln Institute in Louisville; he planned to be a minister, and his voice had grown deep enough, that year away studying, for everyone along Black Pool Road to believe he might.

As a boy he'd been Georgie, a sullen, stocky loner who spent many weekends and much of the summer at the home of his grandparents, the oldest cabin along Black Pool Road. Samuel and Naomi Cox had been born slaves in Virginia before they had settled in that cabin and begun to farm one of the first patches of bottomland parceled out to black farmers, after the war. They'd sent every one of their six children to college, and some had moved north. Georgie's father was a teacher in the colored school in Lexington, and Georgie was his parents' only child, quiet and religious, everyone said, but when his cousins and aunts and uncles gathered on Naomi and Samuel's porch in the summertime, swapping stories and jokes, he'd been known to stand along the edges and smile.

Unlike the other children, George Cox had never laughed at Sarah, at her small size or her awkward walk or her silence. He was mostly silent, too. When another child laughed and called her an odd bird or something worse, and then the others joined in laughing, his soft face stayed somber and he looked at her, watching, as if waiting to see what she would do.

That summer when he was eighteen he'd grown a mustache, and though he hadn't become lean, he seemed to have grown into his weight somehow; he looked taller when he arrived, and strong. One Saturday, Sarah walked by the church and heard him singing inside: "Precious Lord, take my hand." When he saw her standing in the doorway watching, he looked momentarily embarrassed. "I'm gonna lead the service tomorrow," he said, looking at the floor. "I was just gettin' ready to lead the first hymn."

She turned to go, embarrassed now herself, but he called after her. He took her hand and brought her up to the front of the church. He sat down at the piano and motioned for her to join him.

"Don't you miss singing?" he asked her. He started to tap a melody with two fingers—"I'll Fly Away"—and he hummed along, his voice deep and rich.

All this time, and no one had ever asked her about singing. She felt something stirring in her chest, and she realized it was her breath. She had started to hum.

At church on Sunday he preached about the messages God sends his people. "Be still and know that he is God!" he shouted, and when the others called back—"Amen!" and "Be still, be still!"—she felt that rush of air in her chest again.

By the end of that week, she was giving whispered answers to her parents' questions. "Yes, ma'am, please." "No, thank you, Daddy." Her mother declared it a miracle, and George Cox God's obvious messenger. By the end of the summer George had come to ask Sarah's parents to let her marry him the next year, when he finished his training as a preacher and, he hoped, began work at a church of his own.

"I know she's young," he told her daddy. "But I can take care of her. I can take her away from all that's made her so sad."

After he left, Aunt Paulie, who had been driven to the cabin on Black Pool Road that afternoon by a gentleman friend from Lexington, paced the floor and raged. "She is still a *child!* You can't let him take her away from you."

Paulie storming and raging would have frightened Sarah not long before, but now somehow it made her want to laugh. He could take her away, take her somewhere else. He had told her so. "It's best, after all you've seen," he said. How did he know? She'd seen and heard Robert countless times, before he died, telling his friends, "Ain't nothin' in Kentucky worth stayin' around for. I'm going to Chicago when I get me some money saved."

Sometimes they paid him when he played his guitar. He carried the money around in a little sack in his pocket so their mama wouldn't know.

And hadn't Aunt Paulie left Black Pool Road and the entire state of Kentucky behind as soon as she'd met Claude, a man who'd taken her as far away as a person could surely get, all the way to Paris, France? She hadn't been much older then than Sarah herself. Sarah'd heard her mother tell about it many times, clicking her tongue and shaking her head at the end.

Sarah loved her mama and daddy. She loved the way they took care of her, the way they'd never tried to make her talk. Their warm cabin, the loft where she could whisper herself to sleep at night. Where she could hide.

But to walk to the creek now was to see the stump of that tree. They'd cut it down shortly after, for her parents and for her. But its roots were still there, deep as ever. In her dreams at night it grew back, its branches reaching all the way to their front porch.

Robert got away, she'd tell herself after those dreams, in the sounds of her new language. The language she shared with him. He'd take her with him one day, someplace where the gnarled branches couldn't reach her. That was what Reverend Spies had said when they'd buried him: "He's waiting for us there." Her mama let out a wail, and Sarah knew it was because knowing that wasn't enough. It wasn't enough for her, either, but she held in any wailing, any sound, saved it up and told herself, heaven or hell, it didn't matter; she'd get away from Black Pool Road somehow. She'd find a way to join him.

Pilgrim and Stranger

1962

Mary Elizabeth walked down Big Hill Road at dusk on New Year's Eve, home from cleaning her daddy's church. The sky was red, the air damp; she could smell the train that had just left town, its lonesome whistle fading as it curved west, out of Richmond. Ever since she was a child, the sound of a train had made her dream of traveling, going somewhere else.

Money from cleaning the church along with the houses of several women in town—up the hill, across the tracks—would set her up with some spending money when she got back to school. Not that there'd be much to spend it on. Breakfast at a diner with Maze, maybe; Maze never had any extra money to spend. Mr. Roth insisted on buying the music for her, no matter that she told him she had money of her own. He'd sent her home with the Stravinsky. So far she hadn't been able to bring herself to open it.

She'd played some, though. After she waxed the sanctuary floor at Big Hill Christian Church, she sat down at the piano, breathed in and out a few times, then let her fingers go through the motions of a bunch of hymns. She played them slowly, unthinkingly. "Wayfaring Stranger." "Precious Lord, Hear My Prayer." "The Old Rugged Cross." On Christmas day, she played for the carol sing, "Silent Night," "Oh Little Town of Bethlehem," but when her daddy asked her to play one of the pieces from her concert at the college—swelling with pride then, embarrassing her— she shook her head and stared at the floor.

She knew how they'd be looking at her, even if he couldn't see it. Wouldn't see it. Shaking their heads and clicking their tongues behind her back. *Thinks she's somethin' special.* Aunt Paulie had warned her. "If you plan to learn to play like that," she'd said, pointing at the empty stage after they'd heard that pianist play in Cincinnati, "get ready to be lonely."

That she could ignore; she was practiced, already, at ignoring it, the eye-rolling, the tongue-clicking. Her own aloneness. But she hadn't expected to mind the other faces so much. The smiling ones, the surprised ones, the ones that expected her to be grateful. The president's face, his wife's face. Mr. Roth's.

Now kids she knew from high school or from her daddy's church sat on their porches and gave her halfhearted waves. No one invited her to join them. They knew, she supposed, that she didn't want them to.

When she was little, she'd played with other children in the neighborhood. One, Hannah Wilson, had been her special friend. She remembered a sweet, breathless sorrow when she had to tell Hannah good-bye at dark, when both were called in for bed. But when Mary Elizabeth was nine, Hannah Wilson moved to Atlanta with her mother.

Her sense of isolation, of being somehow set apart from the others there on Big Hill Road, had only grown since Mary Elizabeth had left for Berea. How different the college felt from her hometown, from these tattered, noisy blocks between her house and her daddy's church, the train tracks, the corner store. Now she felt adrift, more than a little lost, not really at home in Richmond *or* Berea.

Yet the walk home from the church still felt so familiar that it left a lump in her throat. The smell of someone's chicken frying for supper. The mangy dogs that roamed the streets, trying out every back door for scraps. The red light of dusk, filling the spaces between little houses with peeling paint and ratty old sofas on their front porches—little snatches of a view of the hills beyond. All of it warming her but then quickly eluding her, somehow just beyond her grasp.

At her house, a lamp was lit in the front parlor, and she heard voices as she approached. She could see her mama's tea things spread out on the table when she looked in the window. Some nosy churchwomen, no doubt, come to see how Sarah Cox was getting on. But she'd been fine since they'd gotten back from Berea—no more fits. Maybe this visit would be all right, maybe Mary Elizabeth would not have to usher her whispering, hissing mother from the room. Satisfying those women who came to call. When she opened the front door, she was shocked to see her mother sipping tea and nodding, sitting across the room from Maze.

Maze put down her cup then and jumped up to hug Mary Elizabeth. "M. E.!" she said, "we were just talkin' about where your mama grew up. Elba Helton comes from over around Stanford—remember her? Girl on my weaving crew?" She looked over at Sarah Cox. "I'm not braggin' as much as it sounds like I am when I say that Elba and I are the best ones on the crew. Elba learned from her old granny. She says it's pretty over there around Stanford, but she doesn't believe she'll want to go back there to live." She looked expectantly at Sarah, then at Mary Elizabeth, but neither said anything.

"The rest of 'em on our crew need about a week to finish a row." She laughed then, a little hollowly, as she sat down and took a sip of tea. "I hope it's okay I came, Mary Elizabeth," she said then. "You kinda look like you've seen a ghost."

To Mary Elizabeth's amazement, her mama answered the girl. "It's fine that you came," she said, her voice so quiet that Maze had to sit forward on her chair to hear her. "Mary Elizabeth, sit down and have a cup of tea."

She sat down slowly on the doily-covered sofa next to Maze, who grabbed her hand eagerly. "I've got so much I want to tell you, M. E.!" she said. "I tried to write it all in a letter, but then I just thought it'd be easier and better to talk to you in person. The Christmas vacation is so long, don't you think? I never thought I'd miss Berea College, did you?"

"How did you get here, Maze?" Mary Elizabeth said. How, she wondered, had the girl even known how to find her house? She was torn between elation—here was Maze, right here in her house in *Richmond!*—and terror. What things might her mama have said or done already, before she got home? And what outlandish questions might Maze have asked her?

"Harris Whitman brought me," Maze said as she stirred a spoonful of sugar into her tea.

"Who?" Now Mary Elizabeth looked nervously at her mother, who'd begun to worry the pleats of her skirt with two fingers.

Maze laughed and, remarkably, looked over at Sarah as if she were somehow in on the joke. Sarah looked up from her pleats and smiled at the girl.

"Harris Whitman—don't you remember? From Berea—you met him that day after your concert. The woodworker who lives in town, the one the girls on the hall were always talkin' about."

But Mary Elizabeth could hardly take any of it in. What was someone from Berea, from that other life, doing in her parents' tiny house, in their front parlor, drinking tea from one of her mama's good china cups?

"I thought maybe we could spend New Year's Eve together." Maze was talking again, but to Mary Elizabeth or her mother? It was hard to tell. Now she looked at Mary Elizabeth. "There's a dance over in Berea tomorrow," she said. "Harris said he'll be glad to come get us both tomorrow and take us." She smiled brightly at Sarah. "He came in to meet your mama and daddy, and they said that would be all right. It takes under an hour to drive from here to Berea, he says."

For the first time, Mary Elizabeth noticed Maze's hair, in a neat braid down her back. She was dressed neatly, too, in wool slacks and a red cardigan buttoned over a white blouse. Where were her wild hair and the faded dresses or dungarees she wore at school?

"There's church tomorrow, Maze," Mary Elizabeth said, looking over at her mama and taking a sip of her tea. Those damn country dances again; why couldn't Maze let that rest? "I'll have to be here to play the piano."

"Well, what time is church?" Maze said.

"At eleven," Mary Elizabeth said, then suddenly wondered where Maze's ride back to Berea had gone. "Where is this Harris Whitman?" The pitch of her voice—like that of her old schoolteacher Miss Wright, she thought, hearing it— surprised her.

"He had to get back to Berea, M. E. He'll come back tomorrow. The dance isn't till four, so we could go to church here first and—"

"Are you planning to *stay* here tonight?" She couldn't even imagine such a thing.

Maze stared back at her, then lowered her eyes. "I thought maybe I could, M. E." She looked up then, and over at Sarah. "I should have asked first. I'm sorry, I just thought . . ."

"Maze, we don't really have any extra room here," Mary Elizabeth said, sweeping her hand in front of her as if to take in the house's small dimensions. "There's just the two bedrooms upstairs."

"We can make up a pallet on the floor of your room, Mary Elizabeth." Sarah spoke again, her voice still quiet as a whisper but strangely assured. "If you think that would be comfortable for you," she added, turning to Maze.

Maze smiled. "That's what I slept on for a good part of my life, ma'am," she said. Her smile dimmed as she turned to Mary Elizabeth. "But I can call Harris and ask him to come back for me, M. E., if you don't want me to stay."

Both women looked at Mary Elizabeth now. "Well, all right," she said, still uncertain and a little afraid, but a little giddy, too, at the thought of having Maze in her house for the night.

Maze looked down at her slacks. "But I left my dress for the dance in Harris Whitman's car. I don't really have any proper church clothes along."

None anywhere else, either, Mary Elizabeth thought, thinking of Maze's one good dress, the one she surely planned to wear to the dance, of a cut and style that had been in fashion a good twenty years before. And then the evening took an even stranger turn.

"I think you're about the size of my Aunt Paulie," Sarah Cox said. "We could get her trunk down from the attic and see if any of those dresses she brought back from France might fit you."

So that night after supper, they got the trunk down with Reverend Cox's help. He left the house then, to go to the church and work more on his sermon, he said, but Mary Elizabeth suspected otherwise, watching him smile nervously at dinner while his small house grew smaller, most of the air taken up by this big, loud girl who'd suddenly appeared from nowhere.

Mary Elizabeth couldn't help but laugh when Maze pulled a pair of Aunt Paulie's lace bloomers on over her slacks and did a mincing walk from the kitchen table out to the front room and back. They pulled everything out of the trunk that night—more lacey bloomers and slips, strands of pearls, a pressed gardenia, and several dresses made of a silk so old and soft it felt like it might dissolve between your fingers.

"Try this one on," Sarah said, handing Maze a shimmering black dress with rhinestones at the neck and a dropped waist.

It fit her perfectly. When she walked back into the kitchen with it on, she looked radiant. And almost sheepish—a way Mary Elizabeth had never seen Maze look.

"You should wear that to your dance tomorrow," Sarah Cox said then, but Maze said, "Oh, no, ma'am. I couldn't do that."

"Why not?" Sarah said. "It's never gonna fit Mary Elizabeth or me."

Maze laughed. "Well, no, I reckon not." There was no denying that she was a good two or three sizes larger than either Sarah or Mary Elizabeth. As Aunt Paulie had been.

"Only if we can take up another one for Mary Elizabeth to wear," Maze said, looking over at her.

But Mary Elizabeth held up her hands and shook her head. "No, no. No dress for me—I won't be doin' any country dancing tomorrow." She had no intention of going along with Maze and her new beau. Though secretly she longed to feel a dress like that against her skin, brushing her legs as she walked.

Later, after Sarah and George Cox had gone to bed, Maze pulled a little bottle of whiskey from her bag. "Harris gave me this so you and I could drink a toast at midnight," she said. Giggling like children, they poured glasses of Coca-Cola to mix it with, then put on their coats and sat out on the front porch to drink it.

"So why aren't you spending your New Year's Eve with him?" Mary Elizabeth asked while they took dainty sips, swinging slowly on the porch swing.

Maze looked over at Mary Elizabeth, then smoothed her friend's hair away from her face in the way she liked to do. "I promised my mama and Sister Georgia that I'd be spendin' the night here with you, not at Harris's place," she said. "And besides, I wanted to see you, M. E. I never got to talk to you at the end of the term, and then not even after you finished your concert. There's so much I need to tell you! I've been dyin' to tell somebody, and I sure couldn't tell my mama or Sister Georgia any of it."

She pulled the whiskey bottle out from under the swing and added some more to both of their glasses. And then she told Mary Elizabeth, sparing no details, about how, on the night she had gone to her first Berea Country Dance, she had danced—happily, deliriously—right into the world of adulthood. Of sex.

Later both girls stumbled, laughing and then shushing each other, up to Mary Elizabeth's room. Neither could fall asleep with all they had on their minds. Lying on the soft feather-bed Sarah Cox had arranged for her in the narrow space on the floor beside Mary Elizabeth's bed, Maze said, "M. E., this is comfortable enough and all. But couldn't I just get in your bed with you?"

Mary Elizabeth hesitated, then laughed when she felt Maze tickle her foot. She felt warm and happy at that moment, and curious. Maybe a little jealous, too.

"All right," she said, and then, after Maze had climbed in next to her and wrapped one long arm and one long leg around her, she said, "What did it feel like—honestly? Didn't it hurt, at least at first?"

Maze pulled herself up on one elbow, resting her head on her hand. The room was completely dark on that moonless night, but Mary Elizabeth could feel Maze looking at her, could smell the sweet smell of Coke and whiskey on her breath.

"I thought it would," she said. "Everybody says it does, Fern and Dare and all of them, not that they'd have any way to know. I can't explain it, M. E., but all of a sudden I just wanted it to happen so bad! But I'll admit I was scared, too." She lay on her back then, and Mary Elizabeth felt the stretch of her arm as she raised it above her head.

"But he did things first that just got me ready for it, I guess. Things that felt so good, M. E. . . ." She stretched again, then shivered. "And nothing about it hurt at all after that. I promise you."

Mary Elizabeth sighed. She doubted, somehow, that she'd ever know a feeling like that herself. And then Maze said, "I could show you."

Mary Elizabeth wondered what Vista Jansen would say to that, to the fact that it was her daughter who introduced Mary Elizabeth to that particular type of pleasure—the purring, stretching, shivering delight of that kind of touch. Vista, who, Mary Elizabeth could tell that first day at Berea, had serious concerns about her daughter sharing a room with a black girl. A black girl with a lusty beast inside her in place of a soul. Maybe she was right, Mary Elizabeth thought that night, in the dark cave of her room, in the tent of her small bed, with Maze touching her all over, putting her tongue in her ear and giggling, then reaching a finger deep inside her, exploring there, trying everywhere until Mary Elizabeth surprised herself by letting out a little cry.

Startled, she abruptly pulled herself out of that warm tent of pleasure, frightened by what they'd done. She turned away from Maze, turned her face to the wall, and within minutes Maze was asleep, softly snoring.

Mary Elizabeth climbed to the end of the bed and down to the pallet on the floor. In the morning, she woke to Maze smoothing her hair and her cheek.

"I'm sorry, Mary Elizabeth," she said. "I didn't mean for you to sleep down here." She looked at her until Mary Elizabeth closed her eyes and turned away. "And I didn't mean to make you feel bad. I won't do that to you again."

Mary Elizabeth nodded, her back still to Maze, her throat and mouth parched. She could have cried for days, she thought, and she did not understand why. But instead she sat up and said, "We better get ready for church."

She wouldn't go along to the dance, she said. After church she shook the hands of Harris Whitman and his friend Daniel, a dark, handsome boy she recognized from Berea, then succumbed to one last hug from Maze. Only after she waved one last time as they pulled away, then turned to face her daddy, waiting for her on the porch, did it dawn on her that Daniel had been along as a partner for her.

Maze found Sarah Cox so beautiful it hurt her eyes. Unearthly, she'd have said if she'd had the word at hand. More spirit than matter, than lungs and heart, skin and blood. There were depths of sorrow there, but also something about to rise, about to flutter like a delicate wing and fly far away from them all. Like Sister Georgia, who was heavier, more bound to the grass and dusty ground there on Holy Sinai's Plain, but also about to spin off the surface of the earth. Free at last, maybe, but no thanks to God Almighty.

Maze had thought she might try to be one of them, the spinners and writhers, the risers to some sort of heaven. But then came Harris, the touch and feel and smell of Harris, and she was drawn back to the solid earth by him, held there, anchored. Pulled by something at her very core when he danced with her and held her waist and kissed her.

She was like her mother in ways she hadn't known before. Rooted, planted, part of the earth, of the rich, dark loam. There were these others—her old mamaw sleeping in her rocker on the porch and never waking up one afternoon, Sister Georgia, Sarah Cox—who cut the ties that held them and floated free. But not she, not Maze. Not now.

And Mary Elizabeth? About Mary Elizabeth, Maze really couldn't say.

Through the dark, cold months of winter and then on into spring, Maze's roommate was like a ghost who came and went but never lingered. Floating somehow then, but not so much floating as racing and racing and then dropping—the heavy weight of all her books on a desk in front of her, her hands forever on the keys of a piano. Through the winter and on into spring, Maze hardly saw her.

But once, on a Friday night in February, as they ate dinner together in the cafeteria, Maze said, "You never told me your Aunt Paulie played the guitar, too."

Mary Elizabeth looked at her over the rim of the glass while she took a drink of milk. Watched her, waiting a moment, with a look that said, I'd've expected craziness like that, from you.

She set down her glass and wiped her mouth with her napkin. "That's because she didn't," she said.

"Well, according to your daddy she did," Maze said, irritated. Never there to begin with, and when she was, snapping like a viper, arguing with everything Maze said.

"There was a guitar up there, too, that day I went up with him to get down your Aunt Paulie's trunk. He told me not to bring it down. When I asked him whose it was, he said she must've played it, but he didn't quite recall."

She saw a look cross Mary Elizabeth's face; now she was angry, too. Why were they always at each other's throats these days? Was it what Maze had done back at New Year's when she'd visited? she wondered. Was it the line she'd crossed that night? But she'd said she was sorry, more than once. And "It's all right, you don't have to be sorry, I wanted you to," Mary Elizabeth said each time.

Now she said, "Well, if my daddy didn't want to bring it down he must've had his reasons. A lot of things can set my mama off for no apparent reason. He knows we have to be careful."

"For no apparent reason," Maze said, watching her.

"That's right, Maze."

"Well, aren't you even curious about what reasons there *could* be? Good Lord, Mary Elizabeth, how do you know your mama didn't play the guitar herself? Maybe she's just waitin' for somebody to ask. Aren't you even curious about it, about things like that? Who she was, why she has her fits—aren't there things about her that you just wish you knew?"

"Maybe. Maybe there are," Mary Elizabeth hissed at her between tight lips. "But I'm not interested in bothering my mama with questions she doesn't want to answer, Maze." She gathered her plate, glass, and napkin onto a tray and stood up to leave. "And I don't know what makes you think your mama doesn't have a few secrets of her own. How much has she told you about your daddy, for instance? What do you even know about him? And why do you think she keeps on warning you off Harris Whitman the way she does?"

With that she turned and walked away. They didn't talk again for more than a week.

But somehow Maze felt happy after that night in the cafeteria, at least for a while. Happy that Mary Elizabeth had paid that much attention, enough to notice things about Vista, about her. It was hard not to notice, of course, the way her mama felt about Harris Whitman. It was big and loud in every phone call and every letter. Big and loud enough to make him back away a bit, to say they should be more careful, take it slower, after all she was really still a kid.

Which wasn't true, and they both knew it. She was nineteen already, and not interested in taking it slow. And Harris was only twenty-three, just a year and a half out of college.

But he needed to get more work done in the wood shop, he said. They should take it slow. So she went to the Weaving Cabin and even, more faithfully this term, to class. She spent time with other students, older ones, most of them friends of Harris's—Daniel and Philip, with their untrimmed beards and their shirttails always flapping loose, Jean and Sarabeth, who smoked cigarettes and, like her, never wore makeup or set their hair. They wrote for the college newspaper, editorials supporting the Congress of International Organizations and the UMWA, or on "Berea's Negro Problem." ("The problem," began one piece that got Phil called in for a talk with the dean, "is not Berea's, but that of the poor Negroes who are stranded here.")

They were daring and opinionated—the way Sister Georgia must have been, Maze thought, when she herself had been at

Berea so many years before. When she was the brave Miss Ward, reading poetry to her students, defying the school's leaders and their new, and to her unacceptable, laws.

The weeks passed, and soon it was spring—pink blossoms of redbud first, then lilac on the breeze outside their window, short sleeves and fullness of streams and hikes up Devil's Slide and Fat Man's Misery, though now without Mary Elizabeth. Every Saturday night, a country dance with Harris as her only partner, walks in the moonlight after—and before long, rolling on that newly green hill, their blood moving again, the warmth and the scent of their own blooming bodies making them forget all about that plan to take it slow.

Maze decided to stay on a few days after the end of final exams, to finish up a few pieces in the Weaving Cabin and to be there for Mary Elizabeth's concert. There had been posters about it up on campus, and throughout town, for weeks. Someone from the *Louisville Courier-Journal* had come to interview Mary Elizabeth; her daddy had sent three copies of the article.

Maze heard Daniel and the others grumbling over it one day, standing by one of the posters outside the library. This puzzled Maze; they didn't know Mary Elizabeth as well as Maze did, of course, but they'd met her, and they liked her fine, didn't they?

"Of course we like her," Phil said. "That's the problem. That's why we can't stand what they're doin' to her."

But Daniel tugged at his arm then and shook his head, and no one said anything else.

It was Maze's first inkling, funny to think of it later, that all the attention Mary Elizabeth was getting might not be a good thing. Her second inkling came on the morning of the concert, when Maze woke, as usual, to an empty room; Mary Elizabeth would have been up and out of the room for hours already. As she climbed out of bed that morning, Maze realized with a start that nearly all of Mary Elizabeth's things were packed, her suitcases lined up by the door. The trash can was full of old papers and notes, and Maze saw, as her eyes gradually focused, the sheet music for "Danse Russe," from *Petrouchka*—one of the pieces Mary Elizabeth had been practicing endlessly, night and day, for four and a half months but had steadfastly refused to play for Maze.

Visitor

1943 · 1947

Vista and Nicklaus Jansen's daughter, Amazing Grace Jansen, was born on a soft April morning to the strains of the Carter Family singing the hymn for which she was named. For while Vista and Mamaw had long since branched out to try other recordings—Red Foley and Bill Monroe and others—it was the Carter Family Vista wanted to hear that morning. Shade Nixon had set the thing going. Mamaw Marthie had her hands full with other things, of course, and she'd never been willing to learn to set the needle on a record; it made her too nervous, she said.

Though it was her favorite hymn and she'd wanted it to be her daughter's name, when Vista held the writhing, snorting little bundle in her arms, she found it hard to make a name as grand as "Grace" fit. So instead she called her daughter Maze.

Things took their time about blooming that spring, and the birds seemed to tone down their singing a little bit at dawn, or so it seemed to Vista. She felt that way through the whole spring and summer—just dreamy and soft—as she nursed her baby and dozed with her under the shade of her favorite old tulip poplar. Later, when the air had a little bite in the evenings and early mornings, she felt herself wake up just a bit, enough to chase her exploring baby away from the stove or the steps of the porch. In the winter she saw her daughter's red-blond curls emerge, as tight as if they'd been wrapped and pinned, but with a sheen of gold that gleamed in the lamplight at night.

On winter nights, Vista danced around the stove with little Maze in her arms, and some evenings she even let Shade Nixon play his classical records. Maze seemed to like them, anyway, particularly the Chopin *Waltzes*, or so Shade said. Mamaw Marthie sat by the stove and rocked, trying to find a comfortable way to sit; her gout was acting up that winter.

All in all, it was a pleasant time, that winter after Maze was born. But the spring was something different altogether. This time it wasn't soft. Because suddenly, that spring, Vista was lonely. She woke up that first sunny day and knew it: She longed for the touch of a man. But the only man who ever crossed her path was Shade, and she'd find no comfort there; there were some things a woman just knew. The other young men had been pouring out of their holler since the start of the war, and so far the ones who survived hadn't shown much interest in coming back.

The year Maze turned three, Shade Nixon was offered a job doing the books for a big hotel in Harrodsburg, fifty miles to the west. Something about even his going, about so many people going one place or another, made Vista want to look at maps, so that summer she pulled out all her old books and papers from the days when she'd gone to Miss Drury's school. West or north—those were definitely the only two ways to go, she thought as she looked at the map of the United States Miss Drury had given her on the day she'd packed up the schoolroom to leave. To the east was West Virginia, and Vista knew all that meant was coal mines, and surely more towns that were emptying fast. To the south, Tennessee and cities like Memphis, where a woman by herself might just be mowed down by a streetcar.

Maybe west, then—at least as far as Harrodsburg, where Shade Nixon had a nice apartment above a fancy furniture store and an office of his very own right off the lobby of a high-class hotel in Harrodsburg. Funny, Vista thought, to see the west that way. For her whole life she'd seen the west as dim and gray, the east as lighter and rimmed with pink and purple—because that was how they'd always looked from Mamaw Marthie's cabin. To the east, the sun came up over Harmony Ridge and bathed the valley in morning light; by the time it set, it was long lost behind Pinecone Knob, in front of Mamaw's cabin, which always seemed hidden behind a gray veil. It was the first time it had dawned on her that her west was someone else's east and that the other side of Pinecone Knob might look, from that someone's perspective, every bit as bright with promise as Harmony Ridge looked to her in the morning.

In July of 1946 Vista wrote to Shade Nixon to say she'd like to come and visit, and by the end of the summer she had a job in the Beau Rive Hotel kitchen. She also had a little room, with a single bed that she and Maze shared, in the "staff quarters"—one new barracks-type building and two tiny cabins that were, she would learn later, former slave cabins—a half mile down from the slight rise the hotel sat on.

In the kitchen she cooked greens and spoon bread and endless platters of fried chicken and catfish; there was nothing new about any of this for her except for using more pepper than she was accustomed to. For Vista, most of it was just special-occasion Sunday-dinner cooking, but here in Harrodsburg, apparently, or at least at the Beau Rive Hotel, food like that was part of the place's "Southern charm and hospitality," and people ate it every day. It was tiring work, but Vista was fast and neat, and more than once she overheard one of the cooks or waitresses say something about how she just wasn't what you'd expect of a mountain girl.

That was the first time Vista thought maybe that was the reason Nicklaus Jansen had decided he'd made a mistake. Maybe, she thought, he woke up and realized he'd married a poor mountain girl. Maybe that was it. That was the kind of thing she thought about, standing in the hot kitchen of the Beau Rive Hotel, scraping thick layers of grease from the frying pans.

Cooking at the Beau Rive Hotel meant doing at least two meals a day—either breakfast and lunch or lunch and dinner—and all the cleanup after each meal. While the work seemed familiar at least, it soon dawned on Vista that she was by far the youngest person on the cooking staff; the three other women who cooked were all the age of Mamaw Marthie, and as troubled by rheumatism and other ailments as she was.

All the other girls Vista's age who worked at the hotel were either maids or waitresses, which meant they picked up a little extra tip money from wealthy guests from places like Lexington or Frankfort, sometimes even Louisville or Cincinnati. And eventually she learned, from talking to a maid named Mavis who often invited her to have a cigarette on the back steps behind the kitchen, that on top of that, their hourly rate was five cents higher than her own. She asked Shade Nixon about it one afternoon in the fall, when she'd finished cleaning up after lunch and brought him a cup of coffee, as she often did, lingering at his office door to chat.

He looked mildly annoyed, staring up at her with his perpetually bleary eyes. "Well, come on now, Vista, you know you're gettin' extra advantages that those girls don't get—"

"Like what?" Vista snapped, annoyed by Shade Nixon's unbending loyalty to his bosses.

"A place to live, for one thing," he said, nodding toward the window in the direction of the staff quarters.

"But you know as well as I do, Shade Nixon, because you do the figurin' every week—they're takin' three dollars out of my pay each week to cover my rent, for a bed and a table and a leaky toilet down the hall."

"And all your meals provided here." He acted as if he hadn't even heard her.

"*Everybody* takes their meals in this kitchen," she answered, nearly shouting now. "I oughta know, Shade, since I'm here cookin' them every damn day."

Then he played the card he'd been saving—the one that always worked, that always *would* work, with Vista. He pointed at Maze, who sat at a little table outside his office door, drawing pictures out of a new set of books he'd brought her from the Harrodsburg Library.

"Where else," he asked her in a somber voice, "do you expect to live and work where you aren't gonna have to worry about that little girl?"

As if on cue, Maze looked up at Vista, eyes wide open, as if she'd wanted to ask that very question herself. And Shade walked out of the office.

Later Vista came back with a warm piece of that evening's spoon bread—a peace offering—but Shade wasn't in his office. Instead she found a pretty, brown-haired woman, maybe her own age or a few years older, wearing a pink silk dress and sitting in the chair next to Shade's desk. On her lap sat Maze. The woman was reading one of the library books aloud, and Vista stood in the doorway holding that spoon bread for several pages before either of them noticed she was there.

The brown-haired woman was a guest—a frequent one for lunch, apparently, though Vista knew she'd never seen her in the three months she'd been at the hotel. She introduced herself as Nora something, "Taylor," Vista thought she'd heard, with some other business stuck in the middle, the way folks from around Lexington seemed to like to do with their names.

She said something about owning an inn herself nearby, something about shakers, Vista thought she heard her say, and all

Vista could think of, maybe because of all her time in the kitchen by then, was salt and pepper. Also, she was distracted by her daughter, now standing next to the woman; Nora Taylor had risen to shake Vista's hand, and Maze was staring intently at the long, smooth skirt of her dress. It appeared, to Vista's surprise and also to her horror, that Maze was on the verge of reaching out and stroking it.

You could hardly blame her, really—Vista felt like reaching out and touching it herself; she'd never seen a dress as soft and fine as that, or a pink as pale and shimmering. She reached for Maze and pulled her up into her arms.

"Is this little angel your daughter?" the woman said then, and before Vista could answer, she chirped, "Well, of course she is! Just look—I can see where she got her curls and those adorable freckles." She reached over and wrapped her fingers inside two of Maze's curls.

Later, when she asked Shade Nixon about Nora, Vista learned that the woman and her husband ran a small inn at Pleasant Hill, just five miles east of Harrodsburg; they called it the Shaker Inn because it was in one of the old dwelling houses used by the odd religious group that had had one of their places at Pleasant Hill. Selma, who worked with Vista in the kitchen, told her about them; supposedly they danced in church, she said, and that was how they got their name.

"Funny lot—I believe they've all died out now. Pretty spot, though," Selma said. "You oughta take Maze over and see it one day."

Shade, loyal as always to his employers, was more dismissive. He sniffed when he told her about the Shaker Inn. "It'll never last," he said. "It's just a hobby for those two, Russell and Nora." He leaned closer and whispered in her ear, "Old money from up near Louisville." He rolled his eyes and winked at her before he walked away, but Vista recognized the longing that was always there behind Shade's smugness about other people's wealth.

She quickly forgot about the Shaker Inn, but a week after she'd stumbled on Nora Taylor in Shade's office, one of the waitresses came to tell her that a lady in the dining room wanted to talk to her. When she walked out to see who it was, drying her hands on a stained old tea towel, she found the whole room emptied out except for one young couple. It was Nora Bates Taylor and her husband.

"Russell, pull up a chair for Mrs. Jansen," she said to the tall man in a suit who wore little round eyeglasses and didn't smile. Vista thanked him and sat down, hiding the tea towel under her thigh.

"Now, just so you don't think we're sneakin' around behind anybody's back, I want you to know we've already talked to your boss here, and we have a business arrangement to propose to you," Nora Bates Taylor began.

Fifteen minutes later, Vista had agreed to ride back with them that afternoon to see the Shaker Inn and the grounds at Pleasant Hill. What they had offered her was a job as the assistant cook in their inn, for which they were willing to pay her nearly double

what she was being paid at the Beau Rive Hotel, along with pro-
viding a fully furnished room for her and Maze.

Pleasant Hill was more than a pretty spot. By now it was a
little town all its own, laid out on a neat, square grid with a gas
station set up in the old stone Deacons' Shop and a general store
in the old Broom Shop. All the buildings, most of them over
eighty years old, had been built by those religious people, the
Shakers, and the locals had taken to calling the town Shakertown.
Though a few of the buildings—the meetinghouse, the old Trustees' Office, the Sisters' Shop and the Shaker Inn—were still in
good repair, not all of Shakertown looked so nice. Much of the
land was overgrown with weeds, and some of the buildings, with
their broken windows, rotting frames, and sinking foundations,
made Vista think of Torchlight.

There was only one actual Shaker left on the grounds, Nora
told her—an old woman called Sister Georgia. "Crazy as a loon,"
Nora said. "She still does the Shaker worship, dancing and all,
all by herself, and she talks to the ghosts of the dead ones, or
so they say. But she's harmless. We don't see much of her, to tell
you the truth."

Those decaying buildings and stories about Shaker ghosts
gave Vista pause that first afternoon, but then Nora walked her
up the back steps of the inn—the old East Family Dwelling
House, she called it, pointing to a special kind of rain spout that
the Shakers had designed as she stepped up to the door—and
showed her the room she and Maze would share.

There were two beds, each with its own hand-stitched quilt and featherbed. There were two dressers, a writing table, a big old wardrobe, and a set of bookshelves. With books. And there was still room for a pretty oriental rug, like the kind they had in the lobby of the Beau Rive Hotel, Vista realized, sucking in her breath. She walked over to the window and pulled back the lace curtain; outside, she saw Maze running and playing with two other children, who, Nora said, belonged to a couple down the road.

"There are lots of little ones around," she said. "I guess Russell and I are the only ones livin' like Shakers around here now!" Then she laughed, harshly, and Vista decided not to ask any more about that.

She turned back to the window to watch Maze. She looked the way a child should look, Vista thought—wild and free, happy. Chasing after a loose chicken instead of roaming around a hotel lobby full of things she was forbidden to touch. By the end of the week, Vista and Maze had packed their few things and left the Beau Rive Hotel for their big new room in the Shaker Inn.

"I hope you know what you're doin'" were Shade Nixon's parting words to her, but, basking in the glow of her sudden good fortune, Vista only hugged him and thanked him for his help, refusing to be bothered by his bad temper.

The glow did wear off, though it took a while, mainly because she was so busy through the holidays. The rooms and the dining table were always full—more with Nora and Russell's friends and family members than with paying guests, it seemed to Vista—but

Nora loved the crowds and all the bustle, and when Nora was happy, Vista soon realized, so was Russell.

So this was what old money from Louisville looked like. What that meant, as far as Vista could see, was drinking a lot and having people wait on you hand and foot. Also, feeling free to nose into her kitchen with one more favor to ask and one more piece of advice to give her for cooking the turkey that Cape, the hired man, had killed and plucked that morning.

Because it had quickly become Vista's kitchen. The assistant-cook business had really just been a ruse to get her there, she realized early on, for there was no other cook. Or rather, the "other cook," a woman named Dot, was on her way out—the last in a series of short-term employees, Vista learned from Dot on her first day in the kitchen at the Shaker Inn. Some—about half—had left of their own will, unable to tolerate all of Nora and Russell's intrusions and persnickety demands, not to mention those of their visitors; the rest had been let go when Russell had found them unable to comply with his two solid pages of carefully typed General Orders for Each Day of the Week. When to sweep and dust the breakfast, sitting, or dining room (for the job of cook involved, it turned out, considerably more than cooking); which juice to serve for which meal on which day, and in which glass, and placed in proximity to which plate; the order, and manner, in which the fine china, crystal, and silver were to be washed, dried, and carefully put away.

Vista set her mind to memorizing Russell's General Orders and tried to take everyone's intrusions and suggestions in stride because now that she was there at the Shaker Inn, she knew she would have to make it work. Where else could she go? There'd be no going back to the Beau Rive Hotel, she assumed; she hadn't heard a word from Shade Nixon since the day she and Maze had left.

And as exhausted as she often felt, it was true that her room was lovely, and at night, when she wasn't too tired, she could sit and read at the big table, having chosen from among the many books on the shelves. Sometimes, inexplicably and with no warning, Nora would burst into the kitchen as Vista and Myron, the boy who helped with the serving, were finishing cleaning up; cheeks burning and eyes dancing, her breath sweet with wine, she would drag Vista into the main drawing room, pour her a glass of sherry, and pull her into that night's game of charades. Or, more often, she'd beg Vista to rouse Maze from sleep and bring her into the room, where Nora would stroke and coddle the drowsy child as if she were her own, showing off her pretty curls and laughingly recounting the story of her name for all the assembled guests.

On those occasions, with everyone as tipsy and glowing as their host, they would treat Vista like a friend, a fellow guest—even the ones who, a few hours before, had snapped their fingers at her without a word to take away their plates or called impatiently to her or Myron because they were out of butter or cream for their coffee.

But then the holidays ended. It was winter, and winter on the bluegrass, where Vista and Maze found themselves now, was dif-

ferent. It was bare and still. Snow would fall, but just in little dust-
ings, not enough for Maze to make a snow angel, much less a
snowman. With so few guests, there was next to nothing to do in
the kitchen, and not even any new dirt or dust to chase on Russell
Taylor's daily schedule.

So she cleaned beyond the dust. The inn's front parlor spar-
kled in the winter light that poured through the wide windows,
much as it must have when the East Family Shakers had lived
there, from what she'd been told. She scrubbed floors and shined
silver and read books to Maze every afternoon, and for the first
months of the year she saw very little of Nora, who spent most of
the week after New Year's Day in bed with a cold and a pile of
magazines, then went off for an extended visit to her parents.
Russell, in the meantime, went to stay with friends in Lexington,
going over a long list of typed instructions for what to do should
any guests arrive in his absence. But he needn't have worried; from
New Year's Day till early March, all Vista needed to do was cook a
quick supper for two businessmen from Lexington who rang the
bell one evening in search of a meal before they headed home.

When Nora returned from Louisville, she had a bit more energy. She also had three new dresses—unheard of, in Vista's experience, anytime, but truly beyond belief since the war. And she
had a pile of seed catalogs.

"You know, my hollyhocks grew six feet tall last summer," she
said, and Vista only nodded, having heard this several times already and having been shown the pictures in the photo album
more times than she could count the previous fall.

"The Shakers were known for their fine seeds, you know," Nora went on, "and they grew all kinds of herbs and used them for all kinds of things, even for medicines. I'm gonna make a beautiful Shaker garden out in front of the inn this spring," she said, then spread herself out on the sofa in the front parlor, surrounded by her catalogs, and asked Vista to bring her the bottle of sherry and a glass, even though it was only two o'clock in the afternoon.

Herbs as medicine was no particular surprise to Vista, who'd gone up the ridge with Mamaw Marthie many times in search of tansy or yarrow root to ease her gout or to use in a tea for croupy chests in the winter. But to send money off to a catalog company to order *seeds* for such things—when she knew there'd been patches of lobelia growing wild near the old Center Family House, and just last fall she'd spotted plenty of sarsaparilla and liverwort in the woods below Shawnee Creek—struck her as wasteful and ridiculous.

But so was buying three new dresses in a week or drinking liquor in the middle of the day to a mountain girl like her, Vista thought with a sigh as she went to the kitchen to get the kind of glass she knew Nora liked.

By the time those seeds came in the mail, in three little boxes that Vista kept for Maze, who liked to gather things when she rambled out along the creek or in the woods with the other children—pine cones, rocks with fossils from the creekbed, tail feathers dropped by a hoot owl—Nora hardly seemed to notice them. She had lost interest in the idea of the Shaker garden, it seemed. By April—only a few weeks away from planting time, Vista tried to remind her—Nora was generally bleary-eyed from drinking by the middle of the afternoon.

Russell seemed to spend more and more time in his office in Lexington. Exactly what Russell did, Vista never understood, and it was Nora who led her to believe that "office" was just a code name for something else. A woman's apartment, perhaps, or, as Nora called it, the abode of "some old coal-country whore."

At first Vista had wondered what the attraction could have been. She herself found Russell Taylor unbearably stiff and formal at first—a cold fish. But gradually, over her first weeks at the Shaker Inn, watching him at parties with the couple's many friends and family members, when the two of them still seemed to be enjoying their lives as innkeepers—and even each other from time to time—Vista thought, at moments, she could see it. It was something unnameable, a slow seductiveness in his smile, an easing of his admittedly handsome square jaw. His thin but strong body, more visible in the relaxed and expensive shirts and trousers he wore on the weekends.

And, undeniably, the sure appeal, the sturdy confidence of a man with wealth and power. She had seen this in the men who stayed at the Beau Rive Hotel, and she had laughed at herself, the poor coal-country girl hidden in the kitchen, when she felt a wave of longing well up inside her at the sight of those men in their crisp suits and gold cufflinks. She couldn't even get a dirt-poor boy like Nicklaus Jansen to stay put; what kind of hold could she ever have on a man like that?

Originally Nora had planned to write a book, she said. And she had, in fact, pursued her project with a certain diligence, at first. During that first spring—the spring of the planting of the famous hollyhocks and the furnishing of the newly purchased Shaker Inn with an incongruous mix of lavish rugs, crystal, and silver, with straight-backed Shaker chairs and curved wooden boxes—she had come up with an outline for a novel about a young Shaker woman at Pleasant Hill at the end of the last century. But since her arrival in the fall, Vista hadn't seen Nora do any writing.

"Why don't you get back to working on your book about the Shakers?" Vista asked Nora one morning in April. She could ask that one remaining Shaker, Sister Georgia, what it had been like fifty years before, Vista said. She surely looked old enough to remember those days.

But Nora only waved her suggestion away. "She came here when she was older, after they'd almost all died out," she said. "I won't get any good stories out of that strange old bird."

Sister Georgia *was* peculiar, there was no denying that, in her old-fashioned dresses and her stiff Shaker bonnet, walking along the main road to the old meetinghouse twice a day, mumbling to herself. Or maybe she was talking to her Shaker spirits. Vista had heard her dancing and clapping inside the meetinghouse. And once, shortly after she and Maze had arrived at Pleasant Hill, Vista had walked up a hill behind the Sisters' Shop, where the old woman lived, in search of wild blackberries. When she crested the hill, she saw Sister Georgia ahead of her, in a clearing, whirling in circles like some kind of dervish, eyes closed, humming a strange, low song.

Odd enough, all right, but not a threat. She realized that what all the other folks who lived in Shakertown said was true. Those folks would nod their heads or tip their hats when they passed Sister Georgia, and she'd nod back but never smile, except with the children. She loved the children, and since the other parents let their children drink her ginger lemonade and eat the peppermint candies she made from an old Shaker recipe, Vista let Maze do those things, too. Sister Georgia seemed especially fond of little Maze, who picked bouquets of wildflowers for her and kissed her old woman's cheek without prompting, and without fear.

Was it her affection for Maze that prompted the old woman to approach Vista one morning in May? Vista wondered later. And how in the world had Sister Georgia known to speak to her on that particular, fateful day?

By then Nora was drinking steadily, and she'd turned spiteful, not just to Russell but also to Vista, ordering her around like a servant, mocking her "eastern Kentucky" speech. Even, at times, toward Maze, though every angry rebuke of the child was immediately followed by tears and contrition, then long bouts of self-loathing—"I know I'm a horrible bitch, everything he says is true, I don't deserve to have a child of my own." Vista was growing exhausted by the effort it took to protect her daughter, to steer her clear of Nora's weaving path from front-parlor sofa to kitchen liquor cabinet and back again. They'd had no guests that spring, and Vista had begun sending Maze over to the homes of friends in the afternoons, before Russell returned from Lexington—Nora's worst time of the day.

Still, though, there were some days—days when Nora drank less and slept more, or the rare occasion when she got dressed and out the door for lunch or a movie in Harrodsburg—that were better. Sunny spring mornings when the house was empty and Vista could work in the back garden, birds singing loudly all around her, the smell of lilac on the breeze. Days like that had their own dangers, though—too much time to think, too much time to pine for Nicklaus Jansen, to admit her deep loneliness and her fear of what would happen next. Where, besides a crumbling cabin in a desolate hollow, could she and Maze go from here?

That particular May day could have gone either way. A good day because it was quiet, maybe; maybe busy enough for Vista not to think too much. The fact that Nora had driven into Harrodsburg so early, no doubt to buy more liquor, was a bad sign. But maybe, Vista hoped, she'd stay in town longer, perhaps have her hair and nails done at the salon in the Beau Rive Hotel. Maybe she'd come back with news from Shade Nixon, at least.

Meanwhile, Vista decided, she would do what she could. She would weed and hoe the two East Family Dwelling House flower beds; she'd get them ready for Nora to plant her long-forgotten hollyhocks.

Morning gave way to noon, and since Maze was off playing with her friend Rosie for the day, Vista decided to skip lunch and keep working through the day's high heat. The weeds were thick, the soil dry and hard, and the work slow. When she paused at last to stretch her legs and tuck away the damp curls that had come loose from the scarf she'd tied over her hair, she jumped when she saw Sister Georgia, standing beside the fence at the property's edge, watching her.

"I didn't mean to frighten you," Sister Georgia said. "I only came to say . . ." and she stopped, looking confused, as if she'd forgotten why she had come.

"Ma'am?" Vista said, walking toward the old woman and reaching out a hand to her, wondering if she was ill.

Sister Georgia looked at Vista then, declining her hand, and her eyes grew clear. They were piercing eyes; Vista felt the woman was looking through her, or deep inside her, searching for something. Looking for her soul, if she had such a thing. Maybe trying to count up all her sins.

"What I came to say is that I do not believe Russell and Nora Taylor have your best interests, or the best interests of your child, at heart. It may seem unlikely, but I have money of my own. I could pay you and provide lodging for you and your daughter. I can offer you that, if it would interest you."

Vista stared at her, still unnerved by her clear, unblinking eyes. Surely they were brown, but to Vista, they looked black. Her face had a strange kind of energy, almost a kind of youthfulness; she looked ageless somehow. She stood erect now, not wavering at all, and Vista was struck by how strong she seemed—strong and tall, not the least bit bent or curled by arthritis or rheumatism like Mamaw Marthie was, like all the other old women Vista knew.

And what a strange offer. "Well, thank you, ma'am," she began, trying to be polite, "but I reckon . . ." But before she could finish, Sister Georgia turned and quickly walked away.

After that Vista worked doggedly, determined to shake off the old woman's ghostly appearance. Had it even happened, or was the heat just getting to her? She laughed to herself at the thought of moving in with the crazy old woman, pounding the hard earth with her hoe while sweat trickled down her back.

She worked without stopping, the hoe's blade cutting faster and deeper, more determined than ever to make this a good day. She finished clearing the front flower bed and moved around to begin digging in the back garden just as Nora pulled into the drive.

The first sign that it might not, in fact, be a good day after all was the appearance of Russell's Cadillac not far behind Nora's. Though she was hot and tired and in need of a glass of water, Vista kept working; she wanted to avoid the stuffy interior of the East Family Dwelling House for a while longer. When her thirst finally drove her to the back door, she was startled to find both Nora and Russell in the kitchen, laughing like children, popping the cork on what appeared to be their second bottle of champagne.

"Vista!" Nora shouted when she saw her at the door. "Vista, sweetheart, come and join us for a toast!" And before she knew it, Vista had a crystal water goblet full of champagne in her hand (a grievous breach of decorum, Vista knew from Russell's notes), and she was toasting something or someone—it wasn't clear what or whom—while Nora shimmied around the kitchen in her beautiful silk-stockinged feet and Russell stood watching her, slowly sipping from his own goblet, an unreadable look on his face.

Later Vista would blame the heat, her thirst, her own confusion and discomfort at walking in on what seemed a strange scene to her, both embarrassingly intimate and, at the same time, strangely cold. Whatever the reason—and maybe it was simply that that expensive champagne tasted very good to her—she drank the whole glass as if it were water, and she was well along on the second glass that Nora immediately poured her before she thought to ask what they were celebrating.

"Russell has a new job!" Nora crowed, grabbing the bottle and steering Vista and Russell toward the front parlor.

"I didn't know you were lookin'—" Vista began, but before she could say more, Nora had gathered her in a sweaty embrace and begun dancing around the room with her to the Bing Crosby tune Russell had started on the record player.

And by now Vista was dizzy and giddy herself, laughing as Nora spun her round and round the room, and she assumed she must have been mistaken when she thought she heard Russell say something about "a banking job—in Philadelphia."

Vista poured herself a third glass then as Nora collapsed on the sofa, saying something dreamy and slurred about a house in Chestnut Hill. She drank it as fast as the first two—this time to drown a gnawing dread that was creeping in at the corners of her foggy mind.

And then, just as suddenly as it had started, the celebration seemed to be over. Nora was fast asleep on the sofa, snoring lightly, and the long-finished record went on spinning, scratching and popping, while Russell stood next to it, that same odd expression on his face, staring now, unmistakably, at Vista. She stood still across the room from him, half-filled glass in hand, suddenly as stunned and disoriented as a trapped animal.

For a moment she stared back at him, and a chill—a not en-tirely unpleasant one—made its way up her sweating back. And then, because she did not know what else to do or say, she set down her glass and went to work. First she lifted Nora's feet onto the sofa and arranged the cushions around her more comfortably, as she'd done on countless other afternoons. Then she gathered the goblets and the nearly empty bottle and carried them into the kitchen, trying as best she could not to stumble or weave under Russell's relentless stare. In the kitchen she washed the glasses, disposed of the bottles, wiped up the sticky spills on the floor. Then she drank a tall glass of cold water—the thing she should have done in the first place, a voice inside her said, while another voice, a surprising one, chastised her for dumping the remainder of that delicious, bubbly champagne down the sink—and headed back outside to continue her work in the back garden.

She'd cleared another quarter of the plot when she heard him coming, stumbling even more than she had as she'd walked away from him in the parlor. It was the stumbling that surprised her, not the fact that he had eventually followed her; that she had known, somehow, to expect.

The day had turned even hotter, and she'd begun to feel dry-mouthed and queasy. She stood to stretch her tired legs and pulled the wet curls up from the back of her neck, and as she did she felt his hand there, cupping her neck, gently first but then with more pressure. She turned her head and felt his mouth at her ear, his breath hot and wine-sweet.

"How long's it been since you've been with a man?" he whispered in her ear, still holding her neck, and with his other hand he reached for her side, then trailed his fingers over her breasts. Slowly, lingeringly, he licked the edge of her ear.

For a moment, just a moment, she forgot who this was. It was hot, she was exhausted and fuzzy, still, from the champagne. And, it must be said, it *had* truly been an awfully long time since she had been touched in that way. And so she closed her eyes for a moment longer and allowed herself to go first chilled, then damp and weak-kneed, at the touch of his fingers, his hot breath on her neck. But then she pulled herself away and looked around her, afraid that someone might have seen.

He took her hand then and pulled her back behind the old Brethren's Shop, where Nora stored her gardening tools, and she let him kiss her full on the mouth and rub himself against her. She felt the pressure of his erection through her thin cotton dress, and the one thing that saved her, that stopped her from giving in completely, returning his kiss, using her tongue the way he was using his, was her sudden, horrified awareness that she was going to be sick. Once again she pulled away, just in time to throw herself back around the corner of the

Brethren's Shop and begin to retch there, in full view of the Shaker Inn.

When she'd finished, she looked up to see Russell lurching back toward the kitchen door. And then, though later she would think she must have imagined it (surely she was still fast asleep in the front parlor?), she could have sworn she saw Nora there, in the shadows inside the back doorway, watching her husband's approach and turning away as soon as he reached the door.

Pilgrim and Stranger

1962

They trotted her out like a show pony. A circus act. When they asked her to play, she played—the *Waltzes*, Debussy, the Chopin "Étude" she'd mastered.

They reported on her perfect grade-point average before she began, every time. She was exceptional! A remarkable exception! Proof of something, surely, of the rightness of the school's mission. Virginal and pure to boot. Studious. Accomplished on the piano, on which she played not race music, but the classics.

Mary Elizabeth kept picturing that young man's hands floating over the keys, from such a distance, from the faraway seats where she and Aunt Paulie had been sitting. And yet she felt like she was right there, beside him, or somehow *inside* him, her hands his hands, glazing the keys like rainwater. Fingers like the legs of racehorses.

She thought if she could play the French composers, and also now Stravinsky, the pieces Aunt Paulie had regretted never learning, the music might somehow still be hers. Hers and Aunt

Paulie's. Those years in Paris, that longing in Paulie's chest, in both their chests, when they played. Sometimes, when she finished playing Chopin, Mary Elizabeth sat at the piano and wept.

But a funny thing: She couldn't play the Stravinksy. She knew now that she never would.

Only the first movement, Mr. Roth said, the "Russian Dance." Then the familiar Chopin "Étude," but a new piece here, too, one of the *Preludes*, that also needed plenty of attention. Every day, at least six hours a day—before breakfast, before dinner, before bed, study another time somehow—from January until the concert in May. He'd never even thought of playing *Petrushka*, he told her one day. He laughed when he said it.

On the evening of the concert—a dreamy May evening, crushed magnolia leaves under her feet; for the first time in weeks, in months, she noticed her surroundings—the Music Building auditorium was filled. Invited guests, president and trustees and wives in suits in a light weave and pearls and hats. Every single music student, Maze and Harris Whitman and their friends, all of them itchy in their stockings and dresses and ties. Her daddy and mama in the front row. "Right there beside the president," he'd be planning to tell them all in church on Sunday. "Right there in the very next seat."

What a torment it all had to be for her poor mama, Mary Elizabeth thought at the stage door, looking out. She stopped there after she was introduced and stared out into the big, dim room, the Steinway in front of her, bathed in white light. She stared down at her own hands while everything went silent.

And then she turned around and walked behind the curtain hanging at the back of the stage, then out through the building's back entrance. She walked, her eyes wide open, seeing everything but hearing nothing, all the way back to Ladies Hall, where she carefully finished packing her things.

Eventually Maze found her, sitting in the backseat of her daddy's car in the dormitory parking lot, hands folded in her lap. Waiting.

Sarah

1939 · 1945

When her daddy finally said, "It's the girl's own choice" and looked at her with a sadness she couldn't understand, Sarah watched Aunt Paulie roll her eyes and hiss again, "She is a *child*." Then she turned to see her mama, crying silently, not looking at her. Later Sarah would remember this moment, her daddy's sad eyes, the way her mama wouldn't look at her, and wonder why on earth they didn't tell her then what that meant—being *married*. Being *his*.

But at that moment she only thought of how he had sung that Saturday morning she'd found him in the church. How he spoke to her in a way that was different from the others—like he didn't see anything wrong with her. They were all looking at her, and she started to nod, then stopped; they'd believe her, she knew, if she spoke the word. Her mama could hold on to her miracle, and somehow Sarah knew she needed to give her that miracle now. Her daddy's eyes might stay sad, but maybe his bony shoulders would relax a little, his chest fill up with more air. She'd seen what it did to her parents, when she'd finally spoken several months before, and she felt sorry, at that moment, that it had taken her so long.

Even Aunt Paulie grew quiet now, visibly shocked (and maybe disappointed, Sarah sometimes thought), when she pulled in her breath and started to say the words. It was Aunt Paulie she looked at when she answered them now, when she nodded and pulled in the air and breathed out the first word she'd said that wasn't a whisper.

"Yes," she said, "I will marry him." The sound of her own voice shocked her. It sounded husky and full, like the voice of a woman.

In the end he didn't take her away from Kentucky. He took her only twenty miles away, to the Big Hill Baptist Church in Richmond, Kentucky, and a tiny box of a house, built for them by the men of the church, a little way up Big Hill Road.

She was sixteen years old. She had had her first period only a year before. Her mother's eyes had looked afraid, then looked away, when she'd told Sarah what to expect on her wedding night. It was the day before she was to marry George Cox, and she wondered if she hadn't heard right.

It wasn't that he wasn't gentle. He seemed not to know much more than she did. It frightened them both when she cried out in pain. In the morning he washed the bloodied sheets himself, in a bucket in the back.

The second night she didn't bleed as much. He'd given her two big glasses of sweet wine at supper. Church wine, he whispered to her and laughed, a little nervously, she thought. What would make him nervous? *Jesus's blood.* She laughed, too. Her whole body turned warm, she felt her cheeks flush. She was pleasantly numb. It hurt less then, it felt different. After that he brought the wine to their room at night and poured each of them a glass. It was sweet and potent on his breath and tongue. He dipped his finger in the glass, then spread its sweetness slowly over her. On her lips, on her breasts, then *there.* Jesus's blood and hers. She laughed, then covered her foolish mouth. She rolled over on her side, her back to him. She lifted her hips and let him enter her from behind. She felt a white light all around her. *Robert.* She almost said his name aloud. She saw his smooth arms, the way his muscles had frightened her. She heard his guitar strumming, *felt* it strumming, inside her.

Over the next five years, she was pregnant three times. Each time she lost the baby. The last one was born dead. She stayed in her mama and daddy's house for a long time then. Once again she stopped speaking, except for the gurgling and hissing, the sounds of something none of them could understand. In the spring, when George Cox came to take her home, Sarah's daddy, grown suddenly old and stooped, tried to send him away.

"Find yourself another woman," he said, and Sarah's mama hid behind the door and cried.

But she saw her husband's sagging shoulders, his tired red eyes. Had she made them all so old and sad? Her hopeless womb? All those children gone to be with Robert. Why not *her?*

She rose to pack her bag and join her husband. There was nothing else to do.

She returned to cook his meals and clean his house. To answer his questions with "Yes" or "No." In church she stayed silent, and they all watched her, slant-eyed. He touched her lightly, her shoulder, the small of her back, her waist, to steer her toward home, toward her room. He slept now on the front-room sofa.

Until one night when she woke to find herself crying, moonlight flooding the little bedroom. She'd been dreaming a song, one she didn't recognize. A child's voice singing it, strange and haunting as the moon. She went to him then and curled inside his arms. He trembled while he held her. She lifted her gown. The child they made that night would live. Sarah knew this, from the singing. She was a healthy girl, and they named her Mary Elizabeth, after their mothers.

And then suddenly no one watched her nervously anymore. The new mama. She saw the change herself when she looked in the mirror. Hers was the face of a woman now. Aunt Paulie straightened her hair, then curved it into gleaming waves while her daddy bounced the baby on his knee. Her mama made her two new dresses, with room for her suddenly ample breasts. When Mary Elizabeth cried, only Sarah could soothe her. It was a kind of power, something she'd never known or even imagined.

But the doctor had said when Mary Elizabeth was born, this would have to be her only child. He was a white man, working in the hospital in Lexington, where Aunt Paulie had insisted she go to have the baby. On the colored ward. The doctor was young, and his eyes were sad. She'd seen Aunt Paulie whisper with him in the corner of the ward, then later him whispering to George in the same corner. Both of them had cast their eyes down to the floor when they'd realized she was watching them.

No more children, then. She always wondered: Whose idea had that been?

The men from the church built an upstairs for their house— two more bedrooms and a bathroom inside on the first floor. Their old room became George's study. His church, where he preached a gospel of peaceful acceptance, of quietly "lifting up the race," was growing. He had breakfast once a month with a group of preachers from all around the county.

"White ones, too," he told her with a kind of reverence that disturbed her. She only nodded. White people in downtown Richmond still crossed the street to avoid walking on the same side as her. Having a baby hadn't changed that. White people had also killed her brother. That was what she knew about white people.

But now there was this small being, this baby girl with eyes like hers and fat, round arms like her doting father's. This baby girl who would need her, for a time. Suddenly the people at church weren't afraid of her anymore. If she hardly spoke, still, what was the harm in that? She was the mother of a healthy, beautiful child. Normal enough, then.

Sarah's mama had gone to church every Sunday for a time. But her daddy and Robert had had no use for it. Not long after Robert died, her mama had stopped dragging Sarah along. That morning when she'd stepped in to hear George's singing, she hadn't been to church in more than a year.

"We need to bring you back to Jesus," he said to her when they were married.

"This is the way up for us, for black folks. Up, and closer to God.

"We will prove ourselves worthy, and God will make us all one.

"He is the vine, we are the branches. No one comes to the Father but by him."

What did the Father or the vine or the branches or any of them know about passing a dead baby between your legs? she might have asked if she had ever chosen to respond to her husband when he talked to her that way. Seeing your brother's burned body hanging from a tree?

At times, as her baby girl grew older, Sarah came dangerously close to laughing out loud during one of George's sermons. When Mary Elizabeth was old enough to stay for Sunday school on her own, Sarah started staying home. When George tried to talk to her about it, she stared at the floor and spoke her own language under her breath, to tune him out.

Eventually he stopped trying. The whispering started again at church, the old women telling her, "You need to build up your husband better than that." Black and white both crossing the road to avoid meeting up with her then.

Pilgrim and Stranger

1962

She couldn't be at home, Mary Elizabeth knew. Home was something misnamed, or misplaced maybe. But of course a person needed one. What was hers now? Not her mother and father's house, where now she couldn't do the taking care. Too exhausted, too ashamed—but she could never let her mama see that. Think what that might do.

"Come stay with us for a while," Maze said. "Come to Pleasant Hill."

She still had money from her Christmastime housecleaning. She bought a bus ticket, and she went.

The three women lived in a little stone house, the building that had been the Shaker Sisters' Shop. Half the living space, just off the kitchen, was taken up with Sister Georgia's loom. But then, they hardly ever seemed to be there—Vista always off at one job or church meeting or another, Maze and Sister Georgia always roaming, seeming almost to vaporize somehow, part of the clear air of the place.

Upstairs were their beds. Maze had set up a fourth one, a cot covered with an old quilt. Each had her own tiny room, Mary Elizabeth now, too.

"You can rest here all you need to," Maze said when she showed Mary Elizabeth her room. Mary Elizabeth nodded and tried to smile. No touch now, then, no dark tent of pleasure. How might it all have turned out if she'd agreed to more touching, more time? With Maze, but with others, too? With that boy Daniel? Pointless to think of it now.

"I think this place will revive you, M. E." Maze called her that again. "You know, for those last weeks of the term, you were like a walking ghost."

She wouldn't go to dances. She wouldn't walk up into the hills in the sweet, cool air of early April, when the white blossoms of bloodroot poked up on the floor of the woods like a miracle. She needed to practice. Hours on pieces she would never play in public, for anyone.

"Why are you *doing* this?" Maze cried one night at the beginning of May, at midnight in their room, watching Mary Elizabeth wrap her aching hands and wrists in tight bandages before she went to bed for only four or five hours.

"I don't expect you to understand, Maze," she said, then turned off her light.

But now, Maze said, they would revive her. Heal her with Shaker potions and Shaker teas, fill her up with pies and breads and cookies. She took Mary Elizabeth to the Shawnee Run and made her take off her shoes and get in. They sneaked up the hill behind the Sisters' Shop at night, packs of cigarettes in their pockets or a bag filled with cans of beer purchased for them by Shade Nixon—good old coughing, complaining, and, these days, usually drunk Uncle Shade.

"But how are your mama and Sister Georgia gonna feel about having me here?" Mary Elizabeth asked when she arrived.

"Just glad you aren't Harris Whitman," Maze said. He had visited a few times by then, admiring the Shaker craftsmanship in the old buildings, the beautifully carved staircase in one, the simple, perfectly made chairs and tables in others. Mostly he avoided the other two women in the Sisters' Shop, Maze said. He hadn't stayed long either time, and now he was traveling for most of the summer, carting his own tables and chairs, wood boxes and turn-handle brooms, as far away as New England to sell at festivals and fairs. Maze longed for him, she said, but kept quiet about it. Life with Vista and Georgia was easier that way.

Tuesday, the day after Mary Elizabeth arrived, was a wash day, and she and Maze helped Vista with the laundry she took in three times a week from the Beau Rive Hotel. Their arms buried deep in pots of scalding water, they rubbed their watery eyes, burning from the bleach, against their shoulders while they scrubbed.

"Get a good taste of this and understand why you need to stay in school and finish your degree," Vista said to Maze. "No good countin' on Harris Whitman or any other man. Better to set yourself up so you can work as a teacher. Just go to class and do your work and get the damn degree."

Mary Elizabeth watched Maze's mama warily, wondering what she was really thinking. About her. Was this lecture really just for Maze, or was it somehow on her behalf, too? She hardly needed to hear it—she knew this story, and believed it, too. She certainly wasn't counting on any man. And yes, she was planning to become a teacher, as her daddy had always planned for her. "Music's fine," he told her. "But train to be a schoolteacher first, unless you want to play the piano and clean other women's houses for the rest of your life."

A few nights later Vista caught Maze and Mary Elizabeth drinking their smuggled beers in the moonlight on a blanket they'd spread out behind the old Shaker Inn. This is it, Mary Elizabeth thought then; now she'll send the colored girl packing. But instead Vista took a beer for herself and lit a cigarette of her own, then offered the pack to Mary Elizabeth.

Shocked, Mary Elizabeth shook her head. "No, thank you," she said. Then, "Ma'am," she added as an afterthought. Maze laughed, and Vista smiled over at her daughter, then turned to Mary Elizabeth. "You don't have to call me that," she said. "We don't stand on much ceremony around here.

"I hear you play the piano," she said then, and pulled a key out of her pocket. "I grabbed Georgia's key to the meetinghouse before I came looking for you two. I thought maybe you could play for us a bit."

Maze sat up quickly on the blanket, worry on her face. "Mama, Mary Elizabeth needs to take a rest from the piano for a while."

But "It's all right," Mary Elizabeth said to Maze, then turned to Vista. "I can play some hymns for you both, if you'd like. I believe that's all I'd like to play, though, just a few of the old church songs."

"That's all I'd care to hear," Vista said, standing up and reaching out to pull the two girls up.

It was a dusty old upright, enough out of tune that Mary Elizabeth just tried to forget that she was playing. With hymns she could do that—just turn off the sound in her head and let her fingers go through the motions of "Amazing Grace" or "In the Sweet By and By." But when Maze asked her, tentatively, about those pieces she'd played on their second night at Berea—"That Debussy, the Children's Hour or whatever it was called"—Mary Elizabeth shook her head. It was only because the thing was so badly out of tune, she told herself, ignoring the stabbing pain between her shoulders.

"You aren't sleepin' well, are you, M. E.?" Maze said the next day. Each night that Mary Elizabeth had been at Pleasant Hill, Maze said, she'd woken to the sound of her friend's grinding teeth in the room next door, a sound tortured and loud enough for Maze to hear it through the solidly built wall. That morning she asked Sister Georgia about a tea she'd made in years past for Vista, who also slept poorly.

Sister Georgia pulled a dusty old book out of a trunk behind her loom. "The Sisters' ledger book," she said, smiling. "Sister Mary passed it along to me before she died."

Such a puzzle of a woman. At times, like that morning, she

could look sweet and grandmotherly, like one of the old women Mary Elizabeth cleaned for back in Richmond, except for the laced-up boots and the peculiar bonnet on her head. Other times there was a fierceness to her, a fire in her eyes that looked to Mary Elizabeth like anger, though Maze said she didn't think Sister Georgia was angry anymore. She had been, once, Maze said. But not now.

That morning, all gentle sweetness, the old woman invited the girls to sit next to her at the table while she turned the pages of the Sisters' ledger book. Inside were lists of weekly duties and notes on what was planted where from a century before, along with pages of recipes and herbal remedies, all written in fading ink and in a crabbed handwriting that was barely legible.

But Sister Georgia had no trouble reading it. "Quince pre-serves," she read out. "Sarsaparilla tea. Remember a few drops of rosewater in apple pies and also to bathe an aching head. A poul-tice of calendula and parsley for hives, wounds, or palsy. The dried tops of thyme for the croup." She stopped abruptly and quickly turned the page after reading only the words "For Sisters who have erred."

"Wait a minute," Maze called out then, turning the page back. "What was that?"

She pulled the book closer and peered closely at the page. "For sisters who have erred, try this tea before retiring." She looked up at Sister Georgia quizzically for a moment, then turned back to the page.

"Root of liverwort," she read slowly, gradually deciphering the letters. "Boiling water. Castor oil. Night . . . night*shade*. Night-shade! That's deadly, isn't it, Georgia? Didn't you tell me night-shade's poisonous?"

Slowly something dawned on them, on both Maze and Mary Elizabeth. They looked at each other, and their eyes grew wide. What else could it mean for a celibate sister to have "erred"?

Maze sat back in her chair and looked at Sister Georgia. "You mean they drank this tea to try to *kill themselves?*"

Sister Georgia pulled the book back in front of her at the table, turning a few more pages with her big, stiff fingers. "Well, not themselves, I imagine, no."

Over in the kitchen, where she was shelling peas, Vista gave a nasty little laugh. "All kinds of goin's-on here that you won't find in the official history books," she said, shaking her head.

The two girls stared at each other, openmouthed. But Georgia had gone back to reading recipes, seemingly unperturbed. "Here it is," she said, pulling her little wire glasses up on her nose and leaning closer. "'To aid digestion, and sleep.' I'd forgotten we used valerian, Vista. There's some growing in the old kitchen garden." With that she stood up from the table and picked up a basket and a knife in the kitchen.

Ready to vanish again, Mary Elizabeth thought, and she rose to follow Maze, who was already out the door behind Sister Georgia.

"So that was a tea for getting rid of pregnancies?" Maze was calling after Sister Georgia. She practically had to run to keep up with her.

"So you mean some of the sisters were . . . ?"

Here Sister Georgia stopped and looked at Maze. The look on her face was inscrutable, at least to Mary Elizabeth. After that they walked more slowly, and Maze asked no more questions.

But then everything about Sister Georgia seemed inscrutable to Mary Elizabeth. When she wasn't out wandering or roaming or worshipping, or whatever it was she did, and when Vista was actually home in the Sisters' Shop "caring for" Georgia—though all that seemed to mean was cooking an evening meal that the old woman only picked at—the two women seemed to spend most of their time arguing.

Constantly, and about everything, Maze said. When to plant peas and potatoes, for instance; Vista still went by what she called holler logic: aboveground plants at the new moon, root crops when the moon was on the wane. And furthermore, one should always plant, she said, by the signs of the zodiac, sowing when the signs were in the neck, breast, loins, or feet. Thunder in February meant frost in May. The first call of the katydid meant a killing frost in exactly three months.

Georgia called those ideas mountain nonsense, even though Vista's gardens always did well, as well as Sister Mary's, she had to admit. Vista's answer was to remind Georgia that she talked regularly with the spirits of dead Shakers—Mother Ann, Sister Mary, and Brother Benjamin, dead nearly forty years now, and also the mysterious Sister Daphna, "black as coal," whom she'd read about in the early Pleasant Hill Shakers' *Spiritual Journals*.

"Why do you reckon they've all decided to come back here and talk to *you?*" Vista would ask, and Sister Georgia would only smile, saying nothing.

Late one morning Maze dragged Mary Elizabeth along an overgrown path up a hill at the other edge of town, to a clearing she called Holy Sinai's Plain, to see what Vista was talking about.

"She comes here every day at noon," Maze said, "to have her Shaker worship. When it's cold or raining she'll go into the meetinghouse, but there's hardly room in there anymore, now that the Goodwill's usin' it for storage."

"How much room does one person need to worship in?" Mary Elizabeth asked. And how do you go about doing it by yourself, without a preacher? she thought besides.

"Just wait," Maze said. "You'll see."

It was unlike any other version of getting the spirit Mary Elizabeth had ever seen or heard about. Certainly unlike anything she'd seen at her daddy's church. As she and Maze reached the top of the hill that day, they heard Sister Georgia before they saw her—her feet, in those high, tightly laced boots from a different century, pounding out a rhythm to go along with the clapping of her hands.

They sat on a big flat rock to watch her. "I've been comin' here to watch her since I was a kid," Maze whispered. "Since before Vista and I moved in with her. All the kids in Shakertown used to come and watch. You'd think they'd've laughed at her, but they didn't. It's funny how she had that effect on everybody. Nobody ever laughed, nobody even made a sound. We all just watched, and when she was finished she'd come over and give us all hugs, and then she'd pull candy or cookies out of her pockets for all of us."

Now Sister Georgia was twirling in wider and wider circles, her arms extended. She hummed a strange little tune, stamping her foot at regular intervals, and she looked far younger than her nearly ninety years. Her face glowed with a kind of happiness that felt intimate and strange—almost uncomfortable to watch. Mary Elizabeth felt she had to look away, but when she glanced over at Maze she saw that she was smiling, her own eyes closed now, her face glowing, too, from sweat maybe, but also with what looked like joy.

Maze opened her eyes to see Mary Elizabeth watching her. "You know, M. E.," she said, her voice urgent, startlingly clear and close, "for a long time I thought about signing that covenant, too. I know you'll think it's strange, but if I hadn't met Harris, I believe I might have done it." She looked back at Sister Georgia. "When I got a little older, I started comin' up here to worship with her sometimes. There really are spirits up here, M. E. There've been times when I've heard the voice of Mother Ann."

Maze told her more about the Shakers that week—about their founder, Mother Ann Lee, who'd joined with a group of former Quakers back in England in the 1700s. They shook and danced when they worshipped, and people took to calling them "shaking Quakers," and eventually just Shakers. They called themselves the United Society of Believers in Christ's Second Appearing.

Mother Ann had visions, Maze said. She discovered, in one

of those visions, that Christ would come again, this time in female form. Eventually her followers would claim that female form was Mother Ann's.

A group of them came from England and settled in upstate New York. Their missionaries headed west, bringing in converts and setting up more Shaker communities, including the one at Pleasant Hill. At its peak, around 1830, there were nearly five hundred Shakers living there. They opposed slavery and were pacifists. They gave up all their worldly goods. They continued to dance as part of their worship. And they were celibate, living together as brothers and sisters.

By the time Sister Georgia signed the covenant, in 1911, there were only a handful of Shakers left at Pleasant Hill. "But just imagine," Georgia often said to Maze, "how it was back then—five hundred of us! Singing, worshipping, living in peace, free from the greed and violence of the wider world."

And Maze *had* imagined it. She'd imagined it happening then, in 1830. And she'd imagined it happening, somehow, again. She'd even heard the voice of Mother Ann.

"Good Lord, Maze," Mary Elizabeth said when Maze told her that; she couldn't stop herself. "What did Mother Ann have to tell *you*? And how in the world did you know it was her?" She was sweating heavily now, too. Was it the heat, she wondered, that was making her feel light-headed, almost sick?

"It's hard to explain," Maze said, and she closed her eyes again. "She told me to listen for a true voice. And somehow I just knew it was her."

Listen for a true voice? What in the world did that mean? It was all too much, Mary Elizabeth felt, too foreign and too strange, and soon she felt not just sick but angry. Did she even know this girl who'd brought her here? This girl who'd lived with her for nearly a year, made her think she was a normal girl, brushed away her tears and touched her like a lover, then given herself completely to a man who was not her husband, a man she'd only just met.

"And anyway, aren't you too far gone now to ever be a pure Shaker sister?" Mary Elizabeth said then. It came out like a cough, or a growl. "Or were you planning on being one of those 'sisters who have erred'?"

Maze looked at her, her eyes filled with something that looked to Mary Elizabeth like pity. That made her angrier still.

"Well I'm not plannin' to get pregnant anytime soon, M. E., if that's what you mean," Maze said. "We're bein' careful about that. But I don't know if I'm too much of a sinner now or not. Sometimes I think Georgia's about done with all those old rules." She looked back at the old woman, who had lowered her arms and stopped her spinning. "And anyway, Mary Elizabeth, I'm not sure why you're so eager to tell me what a sinner I am. All that godly Berea talk about sin and bein' true to the will of God and all—are you gonna try and tell me you still go along with all that?"

When Mary Elizabeth looked away then, down at the ground, Maze let out a loud, impatient sigh. "I guess I'm just askin', M. E.," she said, "what good has bein' an upright Christian girl ever done you?"

Mary Elizabeth didn't have an answer. She only stared at Maze for a moment, then turned her gaze back to Sister Georgia, who stood still before them now, maybe fifty feet away. Her eyes were closed and her lips were moving, whispering, mumbling something, words in no language Mary Elizabeth could understand. It reminded her, suddenly, of her mama.

"I'm leaving now, Maze," she said. She walked briskly down the path back to the Sisters' Shop, dodging nettles and slapping at a buzzing horsefly. She didn't go back to Holy Sinai's Plain, during that visit, again.

A week after she'd arrived at Pleasant Hill, Mary Elizabeth's daddy came to drive her back to Richmond. It was a few days earlier than she'd planned, but "Your mama needs you home," he told her.

What he meant, she knew, was that *he* needed her there, needed her to keep an eye on her mother, to clean the pews and the floor of his church, to play the piano on Wednesday nights and Sunday mornings, to be his strong and true, good Christian daughter. At the end of that week at Pleasant Hill, she could see it: She was going home, to his house, for him.

As they slowed to turn off the main road through Shakertown and onto the highway, they passed Sister Georgia on her way to Holy Sinai's Plain for that day's worship. She was talking, to no one they could see. To Sister Daphna, maybe.

"She says Sister Daphna's the one who invited her in," Maze had said. "The one who released her, who helped her drop the burden she'd been carrying."

Whatever that was, Mary Elizabeth thought. "Why's she always got to make such a fuss about her being 'black as coal'?" she asked Maze.

"I don't know, M. E.," Maze said with a shrug. "It seems like it matters to her. I can't tell you why."

"Who in the world is that crazy old woman?" Reverend Cox asked now, as they drove away from Pleasant Hill and waited for Sister Georgia to cross the road in front of them. "And what's she doin' dressed like that, with that little bonnet on her head in this kind of heat?"

"That's Sister Georgia," Mary Elizabeth said, and she gave a faint wave, though she knew Georgia would not see her. She gazed out the window then, her mind racing backward, through the past week and then further back. After they'd turned onto the highway and picked up some speed, she turned to face her father.

"Daddy, how come there's a guitar up in our attic," she said, "up there with the rest of Aunt Paulie's things?"

Sister

1 9 0 8 · 1 9 1 1

She was not beautiful, even in her youth. This had always been clear to Georginea, but it had hardly mattered. "You are," her father had said to his daughter almost daily when she was a girl, "a gift to me from God, full of your grandfather's fiery spirit. You will rage against injustice, just as he did."

And so her tall and large-boned frame seemed well suited to her, fitting for the work that lay ahead. When she went walking with Tobias Jewell after choir practice that first day, it stunned her to hear him say, "You are as lovely as an angel." She had to ask him to repeat what he had said.

By age thirty-six, she could have been what was known as a handsome woman—buxom, healthy, strong-limbed—except for the fact that she had stopped exercising altogether (in brazen defiance of the Berea code) and ate only enough to survive. Large-framed as she was, this practice did not make her look thin—more malproportioned. Her head and eyes loomed large over her angular frame. Her face, oddly, retained its roundness and softness. By the spring of 1908, her eyes, though often red-rimmed and sunk deep inside the caverns that surrounded them, seemed to dance with unreliable flames. In truth, most of the girls in Ladies Hall were frightened of her, and even the Ladies' Principal chose to avoid her by the end.

She packed her bag and traveled by train to Lexington, to the home of her Aunt Lenora, now a widow tended to daily by her son, Georginea's cousin, Tilden Rose.

"Look what they've done to you, Georginea—you've wasted away to nothing, and here is how they show their thanks. You're better off here with me, I've always said so."

Any trace of the wind and light that had greeted Georginea as she'd been escorted from her classroom at Berea that final day, the stunning freedom of defiance and of poetry that had carried her, as if on a cloud, during her last days there, had long since vanished. As she glanced around her Aunt Lenora's sitting room, with its polished brass and dark mahogany, heavy brocade and Victorian opulence everywhere she looked, she felt herself struggling to breathe, sinking back into that black, bottomless pool from the summer before she'd left her father's house for Berea.

Bringing her eyes to rest on her own hands in her lap, which looked strangely fish-like to her, like dead, useless animals completely severed from her mind, from what was truly *her*, she found sufficient breath to whisper hoarsely, "I will need to find work." It was, she knew, the only thing that could save her. When her aunt gasped in indignation, asking, incredulously, if she needed to be reminded of her inheritance—all that railroad money, barely touched by her father all those years—Georginea lifted her eyes and silenced her aunt with her burning gaze. Those strange, unnerving eyes again. She had begun to discover their odd power.

Tilden knew of a position at the school his wife's sister attended, and by the fall of 1909, Georginea was again Miss Ward, the serious and sad teacher of literature, this time at the Beau Rive Daughters' College near Harrodsburg, Kentucky—offering "art, elocution, a conservatory of music, and the strongest of literary courses in preparation for the best American and European schools." Her students were, without exception, the daughters of Kentucky planters—the granddaughters of Kentucky's wealthiest slave owners.

It was made clear to her, during her first meeting with Colonel and Mrs. Bryant, the owners and only other faculty at the school, that the "radical" sentiments she had been surrounded by at Berea would be quite inappropriate for the students of Daughters' College. When they asked her if they need say more, she assured them that they did not.

She read the later Wordsworth to her students, with no particular passion, as they nodded over their needlework. And by the spring of her second year at Beau Rive, she had decided—mistakenly, as it turned out—that there was really nothing left for her to do but die.

It was Mrs. Bryant who suggested a weekend of rest at the nearby Shaker Inn, the former East Family Dwelling House of the members of the United Society of Believers in Christ's Second Appearing. Once housing female Shakers of all ages, the building was now an inn for the public, tended by the few surviving members of the society.

"It will do you a world of good, Georginea," Mrs. Bryant said one morning at breakfast at the end of March. "I remember wonderful excursions there when I was a girl. Sister Jane made the most wonderful meals for the young people, and more than one of us met our mates this way." And here she seemed to wink at Georginea, who could not comprehend why she was telling her this. "We'd ride on the wagon and laugh and sing. It was a grand time to be young. That was where I met Colonel Bryant, you know," she whispered conspiratorially.

A weekend at the Shaker Inn would have struck Georginea as a ludicrous suggestion. ("No time is a good time to be young," was all she'd said to Mrs. Bryant that day, prompting the woman to sigh dramatically and leave the table.) Simply ludicrous, except for one thing: a photograph she had carried with her since she was a child. It was poorly focused and shot from too great a distance, taken by her Uncle Tilden with a new camera that he did not completely understand, she came to realize as she grew older and his photographs did not improve. But she had kept it with her always, from Oberlin to Berea to Beau Rive Daughters' College, as a reminder of a strange trip when she was five or six— floating, as if through fog, to the surface of her mind from time to time, in the manner of a dream—taken with her aunt and uncle and cousin during one of her summer visits to Lexington.

They had traveled by train, and she remembered the thrill of crossing the high, narrow bridge over the Kentucky River, from

Jessamine to Mercer County. She had never seen such steep and rocky land beside a river as the Kentucky River Palisades, so unlike the smooth plain along the banks of the Ohio back in Cincinnati.

In the photograph, she stood with her back to the camera, peering through a fence, a black ribbon in her hair. On her right was her Aunt Lenora, with young Tilden Rose in her arms; on her left an elderly woman with a formal apron and odd little bonnet stood solidly, looking at the camera as if she didn't quite trust it, or perhaps its owner. Young Georginea was looking through the fence toward the river; they were standing near the old fulling mill. Many years later, Sister Mary would tell her, smiling fondly, that the elderly woman was Sister Hortency Hooser.

When the image of that visit floated through the fog of recent events, though, it wasn't Sister Hortency that Georginea remembered. It was the sight of rapidly moving feet and hands, the sound of clapping and stomping, but not of the barn-dance variety, the only kind of clapping and stomping she had seen as a child of six. It was rhythmic in that way, but stranger; she had gone with Lenora, Tilden, Tilden Rose, and a sizable group of other curious onlookers, to watch the Shaker worship service. There were only a small group of Shakers dancing, perhaps a dozen at most, nothing like the crowded spiritual gatherings of the years of Mother Ann's work. But still, those ten or twelve Shakers sent up a loud and memorable ruckus from the wooden meetinghouse floor—loud and memorable enough to stay with Georginea for more than thirty years.

They had frightened her at the time. Yet she'd carried that photograph with her always. Thinking of that trip again, what she remembered was her father's derision when he learned where her aunt and uncle had taken her. "It's no wonder they've shrunk to a dying group of ten," he'd spat out, "calling themselves the elect of God while living in such clear defiance of God's will. I should have known better than to have entrusted you to that woman's care for a week." She'd never mentioned the Shakers again.

Thirty years later, when she woke in her bed at the Shaker Inn, her mouth dry and her wrists heavily bandaged, Sister Mary was sewing at her bedside. Before Georginea could speak, the old woman offered her a sip of a strange and pungent tea—the same milky brown color as the creek—then patted her arm gently and said, "It seems that something has brought you to us, child."

"I knew the river here, and the railroad bridge," Georginea whispered, "and the stream—I knew just where the stream was and that that was where I needed to go."

She grew silent, remembering. She *had* known, as if by instinct, how to find her way to the river, to the crumbling remains of the fulling mill—and later, her mind racing, a blur of rage and fear and despair, to the muddy bank of the Shawnee Run, stained now with her blood.

It was Sister Mary who had greeted her on her arrival at the Shaker Inn, offering her a glass of ginger lemonade. It startled her to realize it now, to remember the strange agitation that overtook her as soon as she carried her bag up the steps and over the threshold of this oddly familiar inn.

Her agitation persisted as she was shown to her room, feeling all the while that she could hardly breathe, and it drove her from her room as soon as Sister Mary left her, drove her blindly, then, along the path to the river, now barely visible below a tangle of weeds and brambles that stuck to her skirt and stockings. And then, when she reached the ruins of the mill and the fence she had peered through as the child in the photograph, to her left, up the river, she could see the high railroad bridge, its monstrous, rusting bulk terrifyingly near. And she heard her own heart pounding in her ears, pounding like the feet of those long-ago Shakers, and in its beating she heard the voices and felt the hot, stale breath of countless black-coated men—Berea's president, Colonel Bryant with a loaded gun, her father's pale face twisted with disgust at her, at her woman's scent and woman's needs, her grandfather's eyes blazing from the framed photograph in the front hallway of her childhood home.

And just as quickly as she had arrived, she was off again, running from the teeming whirl of her own mind, back over the weed-choked path, back behind the Shaker Inn and down another, smoother path. And then she found herself, suddenly, at the edge of the quietly flowing Shawnee Run. The smell of wet mud filling her nostrils. The air damp and heavy, hurting her lungs. The unbearable closeness of it all so familiar, and so suitable for what she knew she had to do. She felt in her pocket for the blades she had taken from her dresser drawer that morning. Without thought she dipped her wrists into the icy water, pulling them out again, one at a time, to slice two deft cuts at the veins.

When the blood burst free like a long-dammed river, she gasped at her astonished relief.

Later, aching and dry-mouthed in a clean, narrow bed, she felt a wave of revulsion at the memory of that sudden flood. Not at what she had done, but at what she had failed to do, at what was awaiting her now that she had failed to die and would have to go on living.

When she had first arrived at Beau Rive, she had vowed to keep silent. To read harmless poems about nature and God to her students and to refuse to be troubled by their ignorance of the world around them. She understood the Bryants' implicit threat in their reference to the "radical ideas" of a place like Berea College. And she shuddered at the thought of having no work of her own at all, living out her days at teas and luncheons in her Aunt Lenora's airless Lexington home. And so she had kept quiet, at first.

Until she began to realize that silence in a place like the Beau Rive Daughters' College was hardly different from nodding through a Lexington matron's teas and luncheons, and she felt the black pool closing around her again, heard the menacing crows taunting her from the branches outside her window and found herself, once again, sick with headaches, waking from baffling dreams.

She began innocently enough—a few poems by Blake, a smattering of Stowe, a few brief tracts by Berea's founder, John Fee. When she saw an occasional young woman look up from her needlework with curiosity—even, on rare occasions, with ap-

parent interest—she would begin to seek that student out for afternoon walks over the college's grounds or a secretive cup of tea
in her own room. There she would provide additional books and
tracts, asking the wide-eyed girl how much she truly knew about
her own state's violent history.

Most of these students kept Miss Ward's strange passions to
themselves; no matter how fascinating they might find her, they
feared her as well and wondered, to themselves, at the true state
of her mind and health. Occasionally other students would com-
plain to the Bryants about their teacher's strange turns of mind,
her odd choices of reading material during their lessons in literature and diction. By the winter of her second year at Beau Rive,
Georginea had begun to receive increasingly strident warnings
from Colonel Bryant and his wife.

But it was Jessamine Parks, the bashful, club-footed daughter
of one of the wealthiest landowners in Mercer County, who
prompted, quite unintentionally, Georginea's desperate act. A new
student at the school during Georginea's second year there, she
was clearly a worry to her family, bookish, maimed, and unmar-
riageable as she was; years later Georgia would finally be able to
smile at the image of the girl's angry pluck when she asked her
father, one night at a large family gathering, if he was aware that
Harriet Beecher Stowe had based the Shelbys, the slave-owning
family in the opening chapter of *Uncle Tom's Cabin*, on an actual
slave-owning family in the heart of the Kentucky bluegrass. A
family very much like their own, in fact, she pointed out to her
father and his assembled family.

Shortly afterward Georginea received a letter from Mr. Henry Wyatt Parks, reminding her in no uncertain terms of another important feature of the state of Kentucky's history: the willingness of its sons and daughters to rid themselves, by whatever means necessary, of dangerous and unwanted interlopers—"be they foreigners, colored, or Northerners"—in their midst.

The threat was clear to Georginea, and now her dreams turned darker still, peopled with dangling corpses and raging fires and, strangely, guns that would suddenly appear in her own hands. When Jessamine Parks knocked on her door in the quiet late afternoon, eager to talk and to borrow more books, Georginea would fumble nervously, tripping over her own apologies, before sending her away.

He had written to the Bryants as well—a very different letter, formal and civilized and expressing, he said, only his "fatherly concern"—and Georginea knew she was once again certain to lose her position, the only work she knew how to do, her one way of being fully occupied and genuinely self-sufficient. As spring arrived and the Bryants' mistrust grew stronger, she felt herself sinking and then floating, her body turning thin and weak, insubstantial, utterly useless in such a world. She decided then to visit the strange land she remembered from her childhood. And she convinced herself that it would be a fitting place for her to die.

"God has brought all of us here," Sister Mary said, bringing Georginea back to her failure by the creek's edge. And then, apparently noticing the cloud passing over Georginea's face, Sister

Mary began to stroke her hair. "God, and Mother Ann, and the vagaries of the world. Only two of us are left now," she sighed. Then she quoted a poem by one of her long-dead sisters with a strange name: Hortency Hooser. "Near on to a thousand have dried up their tears, within this community the past seventy years," she recited, eyes closed and head tilted toward the ceiling, in an old woman's quavering voice.

And then, her voice growing more powerful, she sang to Georginea, who closed her eyes and gave in to this strange music and what had to be, she thought as she drifted, the effects of the peculiar-smelling tea.

The father of one of her students at Beau Rive Daughters' College had threatened to kill her, she told Sister Mary when she woke again, this time at dusk, with thinner bandages on her arms. After drinking some broth and swallowing a few bites of bread, she saw that Sister Mary had been joined by an old man with a full white beard, whom she introduced to Georginea as Brother Benjamin.

"Tell us what has brought you here, child," Sister Mary said when Brother Benjamin returned from carrying away the tray of food. And so Georginea began to speak about her life, and Sister Mary and Brother Benjamin listened closely, and she talked until the shadows of night crept into the room and Brother Benjamin signaled to her to pause for just a moment while he rose slowly and stiffly to close the curtains at the window.

No one had ever asked her about her life before. Now that someone had asked at last, it seemed there was so much to say that she could not stop. Perhaps it was the tea, she thought again, not entirely trusting this impulse to talk without ceasing, this fear that if she stopped, if she slept and woke a third time, these mysterious specters would be gone and she would be faced with what she had done. Or failed to do.

"I believe the thing that brought me here, that brought me to this point at last"—and here she raised her bandaged wrists—"was what happened just two days ago at Beau Rive."

"And where is Beau Rive?" Sister Mary asked politely, and Georginea realized, with shock and then delight, that these two old residents of the East Family Dwelling House, now the Shaker Inn—the last remaining Shakers on this formerly crowded spiritual site—had no knowledge of the world a mere five miles away.

"Beau Rive is a school for young women," she explained then, and because at last she could say so, she added, "Because the students there are the daughters of former slaveholders, men who have made their money from the brutalization of another race, the founders and everyone connected with the college fancy themselves a kind of social elite."

She looked up at Sister Mary and Brother Benjamin, who only looked back at her, listening intently, awaiting whatever she would say next. Indicating no particular feeling about, or judgment of, what she was saying. She had not felt this free to speak her mind since her days at Oberlin and her early years at Berea.

Emboldened by the realization, she went further: "They are utterly deluded. They will have nothing of the word of God, for instance, that speaks against the sloth and waste of their lives."

And here, she realized, Sister Mary and Brother Benjamin were nodding.

But it seemed that all this speaking had tired her. Two old people agreed with her; what difference, really, could that make?

She sighed and shifted her position in the bed, sinking lower into the feathery down of the pillows behind her head. "It doesn't matter now, at any rate. I know they have sent me away for this weekend in order to prepare my things and ask me to leave. I will be dismissed from this position as well."

Brother Benjamin cleared his throat and said, "Then, child, you may wish to join us here for a spell. To take a rest from a world that has led you so far away from God's goodness and grace."

And this time, Brother Benjamin and Sister Mary sang to her together. Their mouths opened like the small, red mouths of cherubs, Georginea thought, though both their faces were deeply lined, and Brother Benjamin's long, unkempt beard was dotted here and there with breadcrumbs from his evening meal. Their lives had not been easy, and their faded and worn, though perfectly clean and pressed, clothing spoke to their very limited means. But the sweetness and purity of their two frail old voices made Georginea cry.

Strange, but it seemed as simple as turning her head, only slightly. And with just that minute adjustment, she began to see again, not only to see her surroundings in the present, but to remember. Everything, every place she had been—and for once, perhaps for the first time, what she saw was the beauty.

And she didn't only see it, she *heard* it. Tasted it. Smelled it. How, living among the ghosts of Hortency Hooser's "near on to a thousand," those lovers of peaches and quince preserves and malt, of the rough solidity of handspun wool and linsey-woolsey cloth, of curving stone fences and sunlight through unadorned, perfectly proportioned windows, of carefully tended gardens filled with fragrant herbs, could she do otherwise?

It was the scent of herbs that started it all, that morning when she finally left her bed on the second story of the Shaker Inn. The scent came from the bedpost, she realized; there, tied next to her head, was a little muslin bag rich with the pungent aroma—not exactly unpleasant, though hardly sweet—of tansy, yarrow, worm-wood: the ingredients, she would come to know, of the Shakers' foolproof insect repellents.

She stepped gingerly from her bed, dressing slowly and care-fully, shuddering as she pulled a sleeve over her tender wrist.

In the kitchen on the first floor, she found a bowl of wild strawberries awaiting her, and she popped half a dozen into her mouth in rapid succession, astonished by their sweetness. And at that moment she felt it; it was, in fact, a strange, physical sensa-tion, almost a kind of snapping, not painful but certainly abrupt, in her neck. She had turned her head at a slight angle, just so, and the sudden rush of sensations—sweet juice of berries, scent of healing herbs on the breeze, sun-dappled haze of early morning—nearly made her swoon.

And then Sister Mary was there. There with fresh milk, there to oh-so-gently take her elbow and seat her at the table, to feed her the most remarkable breakfast she had ever tasted in her life—berries, biscuits, fresh milk with the buttery cream still there atop it.

"Eat now, child," Sister Mary said, patting Georginea's hand when she paused, suddenly embarrassed by her ravenousness. "Eat for all the years of emptiness and hunger. Gather your strength for the Lord's work."

She did eat then, and on the days that followed, and she grew stronger. Unlike the lost Georginea Ward of those last weeks at Beau Rive—where she had moved listlessly through the indistinguishable days as if under water—as a Shaker novice, she sped through her tasks with the energy of a woman half her age. Even after her restless, haunted nights, which persisted, even here.

At night, after Sister Mary and Brother Benjamin went to bed, she read, with equal energy and a kind of desperate need. Now it was not the English poets she read, nor the works of Mrs. Stowe. Instead she read a peculiar series of journals, called the *Spiritual Journals*, recorded during the middle of the previous century, when the Pleasant Hill Shakers, like their counterparts elsewhere in the West and the East, were immersed in Mother Ann's work. Seeing visions, receiving gifts of soothing oils and bushes that, when shaken, dropped pure white doves that turned to angels bearing still more gifts—oils and balms of virtue, wisdom, peace. And, at the height of that ecstatic period in the 1840s, welcoming certain Shaker values in human form—the lovely Sister Virtue, the dark and imperious Mother Wisdom—to their worship. Even, on certain occasions, according to the *Journals*, being joined by the likes of William Penn and the Indian chief Tecumseh.

It was from the *Spiritual Journals* that Georginea learned of the secret place called Holy Sinai's Plain, where Pleasant Hill's early Shakers had welcomed their spiritual guests. She came upon it on a rambling, aimless walk one blustery day in October. There could be no denying that this was the place, though Sister Mary and Brother Benjamin only shrugged when she asked them. "Those were different times; our brothers and sisters have heard the voice of Mother Ann in a variety of ways—that generation's ways are not ours," was all Sister Mary would say.

But it had to be Holy Sinai's Plain, Georginea knew. Two tall fir trees swayed above her head, and the sun's gray-white light, filtered through a cloudy autumn sky, shone on a haphazard circle of rocks as she crested a hill to the south and east of the old meeting-house.

It was this light on the rocks that struck her first; they seemed almost to vibrate in that odd afternoon haze, and she realized that although the wind blew mightily against her face and bonneted head, she was suddenly terribly warm. Sweating, in fact, as if it were a humid summer day, and the air around her felt weighted and dense; it seemed, suddenly, to hum.

August 1845. 14th Thursday, 8 o'clock P.M. Having marched
a few songs, Father William came in from Holy Sinai's Plain
accompanied with a bright band of gold Angels and happified

*Spirits. Said they, we have come to rejoice with the faithful, and
to bless their zealous and sincere devotions; for the clouds are fast
blowing away. Sister Daphna was then taken with the spirit of
Mother Ann, and her ebony skin gleamed in God's light as she
shook out all the evil surrounding her, banishing all the foes.
Beware the evils of the flesh, the laughter of the black crow, she
said in the voice of Mother Ann, and then she was joined by a
host of holy spirits bearing gifts of pointed rods with bright balls
at the end. And when they shook the balls toward the company
gathered there, all were blessed with gifts of sweet oils of virtue
and goodness and Mother Ann's pure light.*

Georginea stood still there, on Holy Sinai's Plain in that
peculiar light, hot and flushed and short of breath, remembering. Something—the wing of a dove?—fluttered by her head.
But when she turned to look, there was only the fir tree to her
right, its bark glistening as if with rain, though the air was cold
and dry.

*Mother said "be hearty." The heavenly Father gave each one
a gold basin to drink out of, and to sprinkle each other out of.
Bushes of purity were also· given to each, to shake over one
another. Vines of holiness were given by the holy Savior to be
planted round the Pool, which was done by the assembly at large.
Heavenly shouts were now uttered—Heavenly treasures in the
form of balls were also received; trumpets sounded.*

She stood in the sacred spot until her heart slowed at last. The light around her changed; the chill of the wind began to reach her bones. When she sat down to supper with Sister Mary and Brother Benjamin that evening, she said nothing about what she had found. The next morning, after milking, gathering eggs, and baking bread, she returned.

Each day she came there. She knew Sister Mary and Brother Benjamin knew where she went, and why. But they said nothing. One week after she discovered Holy Sinai's Plain, Georginea saw her. Actually, she heard her first. Her breathing filled the air as Georginea climbed the slow rise to the hill's crest, reaching over to touch the bark of the waiting fir tree as she always did—to tell herself that, yes, this place, this land, was real. Her breathing and another sound, like pounding hooves—feet in laced boots stamping against the packed dirt, though there was no longer packed dirt, only brown grass and pine needles, oak leaves scattered here and there.

It was Sister Daphna, she knew immediately. Sister Daphna, black as coal—skin gleaming in the silver light—dancing, spinning, worshipping, filled to overflowing with the spirit of Mother Ann. Her eyes were tightly closed, her arms clasped round her breast. As Georginea drew closer, she seemed to move faster, and a flock of angry crows flew away from the top of the second fir tree, cawing noisily, as if frightened by the relentless stamping of Sister Daphna's feet.

When Sister Daphna stopped to catch her breath, she opened her eyes and stared directly at Georginea. She held out her hand. But Georginea felt paralyzed, glued to the spot where she had stood watching—for how long? Minutes? Hours? Where was the sun? It was impossible to gauge the time. Gradually, Sister Daphna pulled back her hand. She seemed disappointed at first, then peaceful, as she closed her eyes and clasped her hands together, walking slowly and purposefully away from Georginea, over the hill and back toward the village.

For the next week, Georginea did not return to Holy Sinai's Plain. Again she slept fitfully, dreaming of crows and wasted fields of dying corn. When she did walk in the afternoon, it was in the direction opposite Holy Sinai's Plain, toward Shawnee Run Creek and the old Shaker cemetery. There, moving in and out among the rows of unmarked stones, she felt disturbed by her own weakness and fear. What did it mean that she had declined that woman's hand?

Set apart from the tidy Shaker graves were a few others, including those of several soldiers who had been nursed by the sisters during the war, when the Shakers of Pleasant Hill had been forced to clothe, feed, and care for thousands of the Confederate soldiers whose cause, in principle, they had opposed. Etched in one of these stones were the words "He said as he died, 'Tell them I am a lost child from the state of Georgia.'"

Rubbing her fingers over the cold stone, Georginea jumped at the sound of Sister Mary's voice directly behind her.

"What troubles you so, child? Why have you abandoned Holy Sinai's Plain?" And when Georginea tried to explain her fear, the apparition she had witnessed, Sister Mary showed no surprise.

"You are a visionist, then," she said. "Mother Ann has called to you in the form of this sister who has appeared to you at Holy Sinai's Plain."

"But why could I not take her hand?" Georginea asked, her voice a hoarse whisper.

"Because you have yet to confess the sin that has brought you here, child," Sister Mary said as she put her arm around Georginea's shoulders and led her out of the cemetery and back to the village, to the old meetinghouse. There Sister Mary lit a dusty lantern, seated herself on one of the rough-hewn benches, closed her eyes, and waited.

And as Georginea stood there in the doorway, breathing in the smell of mold and rotting wood, the encroaching decay of this once sacred building, again she heard the sound of Sister Daphna's breathing, then the pounding of her feet against the worn wooden planks of the floor. Though she could not see her, Georginea knew she was there, again reaching to her, pulling her to the floor at Sister Mary's feet. This time Georginea did not hold back; she let herself be led, and she buried her face in Sister Mary's lap and wept.

When at last she stopped crying, moonlight streamed through the meetinghouse windows with a pillowy light, and she pulled herself up to sit next to Sister Mary on the bench. Then she began her confession. Before the night was over, the two women would awaken Brother Benjamin from a deep, sonorous sleep to bring out the Shaker Covenant. And Georginea Fenley Ward would commit herself, body and soul and all her worldly goods, to the Society of Believers in Christ's Second Appearing.

What sins had she confessed? Not the pride that had led to her dismissal from Berea, not her contempt for Mr. Parks and the other slave-owner descendants at Beau Rive. Not even the rift between her and her father, which she felt—and Sister Mary agreed—had been a natural response to her disappointment in him and others in his position, in the flagging of their courage and conviction, their inability to live by the principles they claimed to hold dear.

None of these feelings and actions from her past would be deemed sins by Sister Mary and Brother Benjamin, or by her, as a newly signed and committed Shaker. Her sin was simpler yet far deeper than any of these. It was the sin that had plagued humanity since the Fall, the sin that Mother Ann and her followers had gone to their graves battling—that of sexual passion, of lust.

The fault was not in the color of Tobias Jewell's skin; it was, simply and clearly, in the unmistakable animal lust she had felt. The animal lust that had plagued her for nearly twenty years now, disrupting her sleep, causing her racking physical pain. The realization nearly took her breath away, and she heard the drumming of Sister Daphna's feet, louder than ever, and felt herself growing hot and flushed, and sweating once again, even on that cold, moonlit night in the unheated meetinghouse, where she could see her breath pouring out in fitful bursts. It was in her own deeply human craving, the longing she had given in to on more than one occasion as a student, and that had hounded her since she had first known Tobias. She had been brought to Sister Mary and Brother Benjamin—surely by God, or by Mother Ann—in time to learn this. She had many years still to live, to make up for all the time she had lost, for all the years of confusion and suffering.

The name she signed on the Covenant was her new Shaker name, chosen, she said, to remind her, always, of her place there at Pleasant Hill. It was the name of a renegade state and the home of an unnamed soldier, a child lost in the senseless battles of men, resting forever on the ground of these peaceful, God-fearing people. She would honor him and, at the same time, always remember her wayfaring status. Like him, she was a lost child, now home: Sister Georgia.

Pilgrim and Stranger

1962

The pain between Mary Elizabeth's shoulders persisted that summer after she left Pleasant Hill, and her hands tingled and then grew numb when she tried to play the piano. By the Fourth of July she'd told her daddy she could no longer play at church. After that she stopped playing altogether.

She slept, though, thanks to the big packet of valerian tea she'd brought back with her. Some days she made a pot at noon for her and her mama to share. They'd both sleep through the day then, yawning and smiling shyly at each other in the kitchen when they got up to fix supper together. Mary Elizabeth tried not to think about what it meant to love to sleep as much as her mama seemed to.

By the fall she hadn't come up with a better plan, and she had no energy for a fight with her daddy, so she went back to Berea. She would live with Maze again, back in Ladies Hall. There was a new dormitory, a small one for upper-class women—white ones, it was understood if not said—where Maze might have lived. Mary Elizabeth, too, perhaps, she sometimes thought, if she'd played the concert. If she'd followed through on her early promise.

"I don't give a hoot where we're livin'," Maze said. "I just wish I didn't have to be back at the damn place at all." Once she'd started spending so much time with Harris Whitman the spring before, people at the Weaving Cabin had caught on quickly. Maze was finishing her quota of pieces in four or five hours of work a week instead of the required ten, which didn't sit well with some of those people, so for her second year at Berea, she had a different work assignment, in the library. But hours of quiet work indoors— no pushing the pedals in time to a song in her head, no counting out rows and sliding the shuttle in and out—did not sit well with Maze.

"Why not the grounds crew, even?" she said as they unpacked and set up their room the Sunday night before classes began. "At least then I could get some *air*."

Mary Elizabeth smiled and shook her head. "I don't know, Maze," she said. "It sure does sound like somebody's idea of a joke." She herself would be back in the cafeteria washroom.

Maze kicked off her shoes that night and fell onto her narrow bed with a groan. "Well at least I'm back here with you, M. E.," she said. She pointed a finger at her and said, "You better not go any-where. I want you right *here*, in this room, or at your classes, or out with me. You're the only thing that's keepin' me at this godfor-saken place."

Mary Elizabeth gave a snort. "Oh, sure, Maze." Maze had

come back from a long walk with Harris Whitman only an hour before.

That fall Maze spent a good part of her time with Harris, and also with his friends, who became her friends, too. They were mostly seniors, and because Mary Elizabeth had no idea what else to do, she sometimes tagged along—like a pesky little sister, she felt at first, though they didn't treat her that way. She spent her days walking in wide circles to avoid the Music Building and ducking behind buildings or groups of students whenever she saw Mr. Roth walking on one of the campus paths. Once early in the summer he'd called her daddy's church and left his number, but she never called him back, and he hadn't called again.

Maze never said a word about the piano. Instead she dragged Mary Elizabeth along for evening walks with this new group of friends, hours of drinking coffee and talking and, eventually, meetings of the college newspaper staff. The student in charge of editorials that year was Daniel Burgett, Mary Elizabeth's would-be dance partner back on New Year's Day. A different lifetime, it seemed to her.

Daniel was a mystery. Sometimes, when he was clean-shaven, he reminded Mary Elizabeth of pictures she'd seen of William Kapell, the handsome pianist who had died in a plane crash when she was a child. Dark and brooding like that, movie star–like. He was skinny, though, and not very tall; he usually had a beard he hadn't tended to, and he was intellectual, so not of much interest to most of the Berea girls. Still, stories circulated about him on campus. He was from West Virginia, some said, grandson of a miner killed at the Battle of Blair Mountain; that was why he was so gung-ho for the unions. No, others said, he was Creole, son of a white soldier and a black woman from New Orleans; that was where all the talking and writing about Berea and its "race problem" came from.

He did look too dark and curly-haired to be white, Mary Elizabeth thought. But he didn't seem black, either. He was quiet and serious, and the truth was, he scared her. He revealed nothing about his past, or his race, even when people asked him up front. He smoked an endless stream of cigarettes, carried around books by Sartre and Camus, and never missed one of the Tuesday-night fireside chats in the student lounge, where Dr. Wendt and a group of students, mostly seniors and mostly boys, got together and talked about books they were reading. Maze went because Harris Whitman still liked to go, and sometimes Mary Elizabeth went along. That fall Franz Kafka was all the rage.

Daniel was in two of Mary Elizabeth's classes that fall: third-term French and Dr. Wendt's existentialist philosophy class. Mary Elizabeth feared she was in over her head in the second one—but it was Wendt himself who'd encouraged her to take it, at the end of the introductory course she'd taken with him the year before.

Dr. Wendt was thin and wiry and bald, and also a chain smoker. Not too long before he came to Berea, the school had still forbidden smoking anywhere on campus, he told the students in class one day, then laughed loud and long. "Can you imagine that?"

He was from the North, from Minnesota, and he spoke so rapidly that his slower-moving, slower-speaking students at Berea had to struggle to understand him sometimes, and it was always a challenge to follow the train of his rapidly shifting thoughts and ideas as he lectured. It was a challenge that some students—like Mary Elizabeth, like Daniel—found exhilarating.

His classes were wild, free-wheeling affairs. It was Dr. Wendt who explained the terms "race music" and "hillbilly music" in class one day. He'd been talking about Sartre, but something had led him around to this.

"And do you know *why* you think all music except for classical music, and now rock and roll, falls into one of these two categories?" he asked that day. The sea of confused faces in front of him shook back and forth: No idea, sir, no.

"Because Ralph Peer, the owner of the Victor recording label, *created* those categories out of thin air, as a way to *categorize* the music he was trying to *sell*, and make more money by telling people what they *ought* to *like*"—here his voice reached a particularly high pitch—"based solely on the color of their *skin*, or on where they might have grown *up*.

"*So.* Keep this in mind when you are looking for a radio station to listen to or a record to buy: Your tastes may *seem* to be your own, but they are *not*. They are being handed to you on a platter, dished out to you without your own control or choice, *not* by any musician, mind you, but by a *plain American businessman*." With that he turned back to his notes and, without missing a beat, asked a question about their assigned reading for that day, Sartre's *Anti-Semite and Jew*.

Mary Elizabeth had bought the Sartre book at the college bookstore as soon as she had gotten to campus and carried it to class the first day, clutching it nervously. There, when she arrived, standing outside the classroom door, was Dr. Wendt. He was chatting with a few other students, but when he saw her, he smiled warmly, then pulled her aside.

"I'm so sorry about what happened last spring, Mary Elizabeth," he said, patting her shoulder. "I'm happy to see you, and I'm glad you'll be in my class." He was the only person at Berea who said a word about what had happened to her the spring before.

One Saturday in October, Maze finally persuaded Mary Elizabeth to come to one of the country dances in the school gymnasium. "Hillbilly music, I know it," she said. "But there'll be a whole group of us, M. E. Why don't you come along just once and try it?"

The "whole group" turned out to be Maze and Harris and Daniel.

They were barely through the door before Daniel turned to Mary Elizabeth, said, "I need a cigarette," and invited her to step outside with him. He offered her a cigarette, which she refused. She'd never smoked in public, and never with anyone but Maze. Inside, they could hear a fiddler play a fancy phrase, and then a loud whoop from the crowd of dancers.

He'd never been particularly fond of country music, Daniel told her, shifting from foot to foot and taking a long, slow drag that made Mary Elizabeth wish she'd said yes to his offer of a cigarette.

Neither was she, she said.

He was more fond of the blues. Did she like the blues?

She wasn't all that familiar with the blues, really, she said.

He especially liked Muddy Waters. He should play one of his Muddy Waters records for her sometime. Maybe "I Feel Like Going Home." That was probably his favorite. Had she heard that one?

No, she said, she hadn't.

He took a last drag on his cigarette, then crushed the butt with his shoe while they both watched. Then they looked up at each other and laughed. She looked toward the door.

"I guess maybe we should go in," she said.

But he touched her lightly on the arm. She was so much better at French than he was, he said. Maybe she could help him with something. He was trying to read *The Stranger* in the original French.

"*L'Étranger*," he said, and she thought he might be blushing below his beard. He pulled a copy of the book out of the pocket of his jacket, and she laughed.

He looked at her, surprised. Maybe even hurt.

She pointed at the book. "You brought a book along to a dance?"

He smiled and nodded, then looked at the ground.

"Well, I wish I'd thought of that," she said.

They walked to town then, to the coffee shop on the main square. After their coffee came, he found the lines in the book and showed them to her. "It's the part where Mersault is imagining being free and watching an execution," he said.

> *Á l'idée d'être le spectateur qui vient voir et qui pourra vomir après, un flot de joie empoisonnée me montait au cœur.*

She took a sip of coffee and cleared her throat. "Well," she said, "I guess something like 'At the idea of being a spectator who comes to watch and who vomits after, a wave of poisoned joy rose from my heart.'" She looked across the table at Daniel, trying to decide if he was joking, or maybe teasing her somehow.

"What part were you having trouble with?" she asked.

"Well, it's just that I can't really tell, and I thought maybe if I could understand the French better, I could figure it out," he said, reaching for the book and looking at the passage again. "Is he talking about watching someone else's execution or his own?"

"Oh," she said then, feeling young and limited. "Well, I guess I don't know." It hadn't occurred to her to wonder about that when she had read *The Stranger* the year before. In English.

Sarah

1949 · 1961

Every Sunday after church, they drove to Lexington to see Aunt Paulie and to listen to her play the piano in her front parlor.

"Only the old hymns and the classics," George insisted. "Music that will lift our spirits."

When Mary Elizabeth turned six, her feet dangling from the bench and her stretched-out hand nowhere near wide enough to reach an octave, Paulie started teaching her.

"No gin-joint music, you hear?" George said before he lit his pipe and stepped out onto the porch.

Before long the girl could play. "She's a natural," Aunt Paulie said, and George bought a secondhand upright piano for the house.

"She'll be able to give her students music lessons," he said. From the day she was born, a healthy child at last, he'd said they would raise her to be a teacher, like his mother, like his sisters. God's work for a good colored woman.

By the time Mary Elizabeth was ten, she dressed herself and kept her shoes clean and buffed and plaited her hair. She fixed breakfast for herself and made a pot of coffee for her mama and daddy. She did her lessons and practiced the piano on her own.

Was she a normal child? What would be normal, coming from her? Sarah wondered. The older Mary Elizabeth grew, the more she worked to please her daddy. A good thing, too; the older her child grew and the less she needed her mother, the harder it was for Sarah to get up in the morning. It was like a giant hand held her down in the bed. The hand of God, she supposed. Refusing to let her rise.

It was because she was wicked. Because she thought, day and night, about Robert. Not the way she'd last seen him. Now when he came to her, she saw the smooth, firm muscles of his arms. Her breath grew short, her lips dry. Robert in his clean white shirt. The curve from his neck to his shoulder when he stepped down from the porch and turned to tell them good-bye. The way the late-summer sun shone on him, gold and warm. The green curtain around the road that swallowed him.

She wanted it to swallow her. She wanted, again, to go with Robert. When George came to her at night, she turned her head to hide her tears. When his heaving finally stopped, she rolled away in relief. She left the bed and emptied herself of him. She scrubbed herself clean. She made herself a hollow husk. One day, when the hand of God stopped pressing her back to earth, she would fly away to Robert.

In the meantime, she watched her daughter grow. Aunt Paulie eyed her curiously when they drove to her house on Sundays for Mary Elizabeth's lesson. So she started bringing along the notebook Paulie had given her years before. She pulled out a pencil and pretended to write things in there, and Paulie looked relieved and turned back to the piano and the girl.

But she only wrote a word or two, then stopped. Let them think she was writing a grocery list or a poem or notes to herself, whatever they wanted. There weren't words for what she needed to say. There was only her old language, the sounds she made at night. *Ah-bay. Ah. Dee. Ahll. Ahl-lay.* Her daughter grew and pleased George and did not need her, and she spoke a language no one knew. No one but Robert.

The summer day when a neighbor found her gasping and gagging in his barn, she couldn't find a way to tell them that mostly she had tied the rope because she was curious. To see what it might feel like. She hadn't necessarily hoped to die, then. Now the churchwomen all watched her with real fear. And this girl, the young woman who played Chopin and Ravel and "I'll Fly Away"? Sarah hardly knew her. George took the girl to the home of a neighbor, a woman from the church, when she started to bleed. Let her be the one to tell Mary Elizabeth what her mama had told her the night before her wedding, Sarah thought. There was nothing to say, really, to prepare a girl for all that was about. But she tried to tell her daughter more with her eyes: Don't be fooled by how a man can make you feel.

Ah. Say-eee. Ah-bay. Ah-dee.

Mary Elizabeth, dutiful girl. Her eyes worried back. Her hands then on Sarah's shoulders, pulling her, steering her toward her room. "Let's take you up to lie down a while, Mama." George had taught her to do that whenever Sarah started to speak the words they didn't understand. When she tried to push off the heavy weight of God's hand. Like her husband's suffocating weight at night.

Sarah did feel sorry to have caused so many people so much worry through the years. When her daddy had died, a year after Mary Elizabeth was born, she'd almost felt relieved. No more looking into those sad eyes, like two bruises. Two years later her mama was dead, too, and ten years after that, Aunt Paulie. Sarah watched her daughter for signs of sadness, but if Mary Elizabeth cried, she did not see it. After that George drove his daughter to Lexington, for a lesson with someone Paulie had known at the university, every Saturday.

At the end of the summer after Mary Elizabeth graduated from high school, she packed her bags to leave for Berea College, the place George Cox had planned for his daughter to attend since the day it had reopened its doors to black students, in 1950. That fall of 1961, Mary Elizabeth would be one of a dozen black students in the freshman class. Sarah nearly choked when she thought of it, the air suddenly gone from her lungs.

"You need to come along and do your best," George said to her on the Saturday morning they were to drive Mary Elizabeth to the college. "You need to do this for your girl."

And so she went, and she did her best to be the way they

wanted her to be. She shook the roommate's mother's hand. She reminded herself to keep on breathing. She kept her eye on the door.

All the while, that roommate watched her. That fearless, smiling white girl and her unrelenting gaze. Maze. What kind of a name was that? Puzzle, mystery, lots of ways in and no way out.

It rained hard during the whole ride home to Richmond. Neither she nor George said a word. Another child gone, she thought, over and over. Away and gone for good. *Ah-bay. Oh. I been, I seen. Robert, I been and I seen and I am lost—tell me: where is our home?*

Pilgrim and Stranger
1962

In the end Mary Elizabeth never got to listen to Daniel's Muddy Waters records. They were both so busy, she tried explaining to Maze, who'd wanted every detail about that night when she and Daniel never made it through the door to the country dance.

"But wouldn't you like to go out with him again, Mary Elizabeth?" Maze asked her the next day, and several times after that. "Don't you like him?"

"Well, sure I do," Mary Elizabeth said. Though the truth was, she was afraid of Daniel. He was too smart, she thought, too mysterious—and surely not really interested in her. Sometimes she tried to imagine bringing him home to meet her mama and daddy, but found that she couldn't.

Also, by the middle of the term she was preoccupied with other things. One day Dr. Wendt asked her to come talk to him in his office. "Are you happy here at Berea, Mary Elizabeth?" he asked her.

"Happy?" she said, and before she could figure out how to answer that question, he was off and running, talking fast. The Northern way.

Because, he said, it seemed to him she might be better off at a different kind of school. Someplace larger, better, a place that could offer her more—in the North. For instance, he himself was a graduate of the University of Chicago. He knew of a scholarship for students there, one she was qualified for. He would be glad to recommend her for it. He had all the application materials right there, as a matter of fact, if she was interested. She would need to write a thorough, polished essay as part of her application. He might suggest an expanded and more fully researched version of her paper on Sartre's *Anti-Semite and Jew* from earlier in the semester. He would be happy to help her work on it.

The next day, without thinking more about it and without telling anyone what she was doing, Mary Elizabeth sat down in the library to get to work. She pulled out as many books on Sartre as she could find, and she worked right through dinner and nearly forgot to go to work in the kitchen washroom.

As she rinsed and stacked the dishes that night, she imagined herself as a scholarship student somewhere else. In *Chicago*. The only city of any size she'd been to was Cincinnati, and then only for an evening, for the concert Aunt Paulie had taken her to when she was twelve.

Her fingers tingled, then ached, but she suppressed the desire—to find a piano and start to play—that always came over her when she felt happy or excited.

This was surely it, she told herself—what she was meant to do, a reasonable thing to reach for, unlike the foolish thing she'd tried to reach for the year before. That night, as she crawled into her bed with a book, she noticed that for the first time in weeks, maybe even in months, the pain between her shoulders was gone.

She made slow, steady progress on her essay, working on it during the weeks that followed, shyly handing over drafts to Dr. Wendt and taking careful notes as he made suggestions. On the weekends she excused herself when Maze, Harris, and the others invited her along for hikes or parties. Then, as the end of the term approached, she put the application aside for a while; it wasn't due until the end of January, and she had papers to write and exams to study for.

On the morning of her last final exam, the one for Dr. Wendt's class, Mary Elizabeth's daddy showed up on campus and called up to her room.

She gave him a brisk hug, then asked why he'd come so early. "I thought you weren't coming for me until tomorrow," she said. "I've got my last final today, in just a couple hours."

"We had to take your mama to the hospital again, Mary Elizabeth," he said. "I'd like you to come home today."

She packed her bag quickly and left a note for Maze, and her daddy waited in the car while she went to take her exam.

Later, riding next to her father and flushed with the awareness that she'd done very well on Dr. Wendt's exam, she thought of saying something about her application to the University of

Chicago. But first she asked about her mama. He'd found her in the church basement three days before, her daddy said. Twisting and gagging at the end of a knotted piece of clothesline rope.

By the time Mary Elizabeth saw her mama, she'd been released from the hospital and moved to the county home outside Stanford, known to everyone in the area as the Colored Home. She was visited there every day by her childhood friend Clarisa Pool. Clarisa had never married, and she lived now in a little house in Stanford and worked as a nurse at the hospital in Richmond; that was how she'd found out about what had happened to Sarah Cox since their childhoods together along Black Pool Road, outside Stanford.

Since she didn't have a car to get over to see her mama, Mary Elizabeth stayed with Clarisa for most of the Christmas break. George Cox drove over when he could; there was a lot to tend to at home, he said. After services on Christmas day, which Mary Elizabeth declined to attend, he drove to Stanford with a sweater for Mary Elizabeth and a necklace for her mother.

Mary Elizabeth opened the gift for her mother, then fastened the necklace around her neck. "Isn't it pretty, Mama?" she said. But Sarah gave no sign of noticing.

The Colored Home was not quite as awful as Mary Elizabeth had expected; it was clean and bright with sunlight, and in every room there were at least a few people who were alert enough to be playing cards or telling stories, though the storytellers generally seemed to be speaking to themselves. Clean as it was, though, every corner smelled of old age—that kind of half-sour, half-sweet, on-the-edge-of-rotting smell that, Mary Elizabeth knew from helping care for the frail old mother of one of the white women she'd cleaned for the summer before, makes no distinction based on race.

Sarah Cox was a good thirty years younger than any of the other folks in that home, but you wouldn't have known it to look at her. Her hair, which she had always carefully braided and then pinned discreetly at the nape of her neck, had gone frizzy and streaked with gray, and her skin was dry and ashen. She was thinner than before, which hardly seemed possible, and the first time Mary Elizabeth saw her she had to step outside the building and cry.

She seemed not to know her daughter. Each time they visited, Clarisa Pool would push Mary Elizabeth toward her mother. "Here's your girl, Sarah," she shouted. "Here's your beautiful girl come from college to see you."

Sometimes Sarah nodded ever so slightly before she turned her glassy eyes back to the handkerchief that she held in her lap, knotting and unknotting it, over and over again.

On the last day of Mary Elizabeth's Christmas vacation, standing in the hallway outside her mama's room, her daddy told her that her mama would be staying there for a while. "I can't take care of her on my own," he said. "I'm afraid to leave her in the house by herself." He wouldn't listen when Mary Elizabeth offered to stay home to care for her. He held up a hand to stop her.

"You've got work to do back at Berea," he said. She said nothing about her application for the University of Chicago scholarship, untouched for weeks now.

Later, when Clarisa Pool got off work, she came to help feed Sarah her dinner. When she and Mary Elizabeth had gotten Sarah settled for the night, they walked back to Clarisa's house through a bitter wind.

"What in God's name has happened to her?" Mary Elizabeth blurted out, choking through a sudden rush of tears.

Clarisa stopped and looked over at Mary Elizabeth curiously. "You don't know much about her, do you?" she said.

Mary Elizabeth swallowed her tears and tried to put on the dignified face she knew her daddy would want her to wear. "You mean about her fits? I know all about her fits—I was the one who walked her up to bed every time she started on one," she said, trying to keep her voice steady. It infuriated her to hear this woman, who hadn't really known Sarah Cox since she was a child, implying that she didn't know her own mother after all those years of caring for her, struggling, along with her daddy, to keep her bouts of senseless whispering and her jags of crying in her bedroom hidden from the rest of the world.

"Her 'fits'?" Clarisa said then, her broad face contorted by a peculiar kind of smile. She shook her head, "No, child, I'm not talkin' 'bout any kind of 'fits.'"

Mary Elizabeth looked down at the ground as she walked.

"I know she's tried to kill herself more than once now, if that's what you mean."

Clarisa shook her head again and clicked her tongue. "Law, girl," she said. "He hasn't told you a thing, has he?"

And that day, walking away from the Stanford Colored Home through a blustery wind carrying random snowflakes, Mary Elizabeth learned, for the first time in her life and from an actual witness, about her mama's younger, happier life. A life of sunshine and music, according to Clarisa Pool, spent running over grassy fields with Clarisa and her brothers, catching crawdads in the creek near their families' cabins, listening to stories and songs by the fire at night. Like her, Sarah helped her mama in the kitchen, Clarisa said, then waited for her daddy and her big brother, a sweet-faced boy who played the guitar, to get back from the fields.

But that all changed for Sarah Cox on a sunny morning in 1935 when, walking down to the creek from her family's cabin, she came across the badly burned body of her eighteen-year-old brother, hanging from a rope tied around a tree limb at the edge of the dirt road.

"I suppose she didn't even know what it was at first," Clarisa said. "They told us later that the only part of him that wasn't burned beyond recognition was his face."

"Who did that to him?" Mary Elizabeth asked, not even feeling the wind that made them hold tight to their whipping coats and scarves.

"Prob'ly a group of drunk boys from Lexington who'd been down at the bar where he was playin' that night. Nobody ever caught them."

Some time later it would appall Mary Elizabeth, remembering this conversation, to hear herself asking the question she asked next. "Why'd they do it to him—what had he done?" But that was what her daddy had taught her, and everyone else at the Big Hill Christian Church in Richmond. Such things happened, yes. But the Lord looked after those who lived in righteousness and asked for his guidance. Only Negroes who talked back or stepped out of line risked such dangers, George assured his congregation. If they kept to their own and minded their tongues, they would be safe.

Clarisa seemed unsurprised by the question. She looked over at Mary Elizabeth with a strange, almost pitying, look on her face, then turned and started walking again. "I don't imagine he'd done a thing," she said between clenched teeth.

For the rest of the walk back to Clarisa's house, Mary Elizabeth gathered her coat around herself as tightly as she could. She wasn't sure she believed Clarisa Pool. Not her, she kept thinking. Not her family.

And yet hadn't she always known, somehow? The tears in Aunt Paulie's eyes that night in Cincinnati, after the concert. Mary Elizabeth had thought it was because she wished it were her there on that stage, playing. Then the look on her face when Mary Elizabeth had looked into her aunt's eyes and asked, "Why

did you come back here? Why didn't you stay in Paris to study
and play more?"

Aunt Paulie had put her hand over her mouth and choked
back a sob. It frightened Mary Elizabeth to see her like that, but
she tried not to show it; she was twelve by then, nearly a woman,
strong and good.

"Because of your mama," Aunt Paulie was saying, whispering
it into her hand. "Because of Robert . . ." She looked at Mary
Elizabeth, her eyes suddenly wide, startled, then abruptly stopped.
She pulled Mary Elizabeth into a tight hug, then released her
and gathered her sweater and bag. "Let's go," she said, "or we'll miss
our bus."

Mary Elizabeth never asked her what she'd meant that day.
She knew she wasn't meant to ask. Her mama's brother, Robert,
had died when Sarah was twelve, the age Mary Elizabeth was
then, and it broke her mama's heart, her daddy had told her; it
wasn't something they should talk about.

She wasn't to ask more questions. She was twelve and nearly
a woman. Strong and good. And she was going to play the piano
like that man she'd just watched on stage.

Aunt Paulie died six months later.

Now Clarisa was struggling to keep up with Mary Elizabeth,
who could hear the heavy woman's ragged breaths behind her. "I
know he thinks it was better for you not to know," she was saying.
"And I could see that, for a time. But you're old enough to know
now. There's no point in lyin' about it anymore."

Mary Elizabeth hunched her shoulders. The stabbing pain came back, suddenly, as they walked through Clarisa's front door, then stepped out of their galoshes and hung up their coats and scarves. Clarisa was talking again, the door barely closed behind them before she started. Mary Elizabeth tried not to listen, but she couldn't tune her out. "Your daddy married your mama when she was hardly more than a girl. He was already a preacher by then, and he had his church over in Richmond."

Clarisa paused to take off her glasses, wiped them on her blouse, then put them on again. Maybe that was it, Mary Elizabeth thought; maybe she couldn't see well enough to look into Mary Elizabeth's eyes. Which were surely pleading as much as she was pleading inside, for the woman to stop, not to tell her any more.

"What your daddy said to your mama's daddy was that he wanted to take her away from Black Pool Road before all that sorrow ate her alive," Clarisa went on. "And your mama's daddy agreed to let her go. The truth is, after he'd gone off and studied to be a preacher, your daddy didn't much approve of your mama's family, especially on your granddaddy's side. His sister, your Aunt Paulie, she'd come back from Paris and declared she'd never set foot inside a church again. I imagine your daddy was scandalized by her, but he couldn't get to Sarah without dealin' with her. Paulie saw to that.

"But your mama was nothin' like Paulie," Clarisa said then, her voice suddenly soft. "She was shy and sweet all along, even when she turned peculiar and wouldn't talk for all those years."

Here she paused and looked closely at Mary Elizabeth. "You take after both of them," she said, "your mama and her mama, and of course your daddy, too. Though every now and again, I think I can catch a little somethin' in your eyes that reminds me of your mama's daddy. Poor old Mr. Henry. The sorrow he had to live through, first to lose Robert and then all the troubles with your mama . . ."

Mary Elizabeth braced herself for more horrors. Would there ever be an end to Clarisa's tale? She felt dizzy, and a little sick, and she leaned against the wall to steady herself.

"Your mama's heart was broken more than once, child," Clarisa said, and shook her head. "They say she lost more than one baby before you were born. And then her daddy died, and her mama not long after that. Do you even remember your granny, Mary Elizabeth?"

"Barely," Mary Elizabeth whispered. She had vague memories of an old woman in old-fashioned country clothes, a tiny cabin, and a wooden porch with a floor that was painted blue, where she'd played with a china doll of her mother's. She'd never seen that doll since. That grandmother had died when she was three, and they had never gone back to that rundown row of cabins on Black Pool Road again. After that they visited only Aunt Paulie and her Grandmother Cox in Lexington, both of whom were dead by the time Mary Elizabeth started high school.

They were still standing by Clarisa's front door, next to the rack where they'd hung their coats. All Mary Elizabeth wanted was to lie down somewhere and fall asleep.

"Your granddaddy bought a gun after they did that to Robert," Clarisa was saying now. "I believe that's what made your daddy want to get your mama away from there, as much as her sadness."

Now she walked further into the house, pausing to turn on a lamp on a table by the door. "So it's more sad than ever, I guess, to see what's happened to Sarah. Even with your daddy takin' her away and givin' her a nice house and havin' you, even with all that, she's still been eaten up by that sadness, Mary Elizabeth. Ever since. But it's been a long, slow thing. A long, slow thing gnawin' on her, like some old dog with a dried-up bone."

She turned then to see Mary Elizabeth still leaning against the wall by the front door. "Are you all right?" she asked.

"I'm just gonna go lie down," Mary Elizabeth said.

Put that out of your mind, now, Mary Elizabeth heard a voice in her head say as she collapsed onto Clarisa's living room sofa. Probably it was her own voice, though she told herself, for a long time afterward, when she continued to hear it—*Put that out of your mind*—that it was her daddy's voice. She woke in the middle of the night, tangled in a blanket, sweating. The first thing she thought of was the last thing Clarisa had said to her the evening before: "A long, slow thing gnawin' on her, like some old dog with a dried-up bone." For a moment she caught a glimpse of something, maybe something she'd dreamed: an angry dog, inches from her face, its fangs bared.

The next morning her daddy arrived to drive her back to Berea. A week after she returned, she mailed her scholarship application, along with Dr. Wendt's letter of recommendation, to the University of Chicago.

Put that out of your mind, she thought, remembering the angry dog in her dream. And then, for some reason, she thought of that passage from *The Stranger*. *Un flot de joie empoisonnée. Un flot de joie empoisonnée me montait au cœur.* "A wave of poisoned joy rose from my heart." Who was watching and who was dying at *that* execution, when the uncle she'd never known was killed?

Pilgrim and Stranger

1 9 6 3

There was a war, with talk of conscription. There was Mary Elizabeth planning to go off to Chicago; Maze had seen the application on her desk months before. There was Vista claiming Sister Georgia didn't need her and threatening to leave Pleasant Hill, going out with some divorced man from Harrodsburg. ("Aren't you the righteous maiden?" Mary Elizabeth said when Maze expressed disapproval.)

Harris worrying about the future, not even cheered by the dances anymore.

And she, Maze, could find no helpful answers in the books they told her to read, in the chapel services they expected her to attend, not even when she went back to Pleasant Hill for a weekend and climbed up to Holy Sinai's Plain with Sister Georgia. Somehow the wind had gone out of Sister Georgia's sails, too.

And now, in the midst of all these things, why should Maze finish college just so she could become a teacher? What in the world did she have to teach anyone?

So one night in February, while her friends were sprawled around the student lounge after one of Dr. Wendt's fireside lounge discussions, she proposed an idea she'd had for a while.

"I mean it," she said. "We could do it. We could move to Pleasant Hill and look after Sister Georgia. We could follow the old Shaker ways—get some chickens and a cow, plow up the old kitchen garden and plant it again, preserve what we grow for the winter. Live off the land, or at least the piece of it that's still in Sister Georgia's name."

Here she was claiming more than she actually knew; it had never been clear to her who actually owned what at Pleasant Hill. Whenever Vista had asked her about it, Sister Georgia had only said, "The land is God's. It's not ours to own."

But it didn't matter what she said, she supposed. They weren't likely to take her seriously.

And where did she get such far-fetched ideas anyway? Probably from Sister Georgia, from her stories about the early Shakers. Maze had been listening hard, for a while now, for the true voice of Mother Ann. Late one night the week before, as she'd sat shivering at a loom in the Weaving Cabin, moonlight pouring through the window beside her, it had come to her: They could *all* go back to Pleasant Hill.

Vista, Maze knew, would've laughed her hard-edged, angry laugh to hear Maze talk in the fireside lounge that evening. Maze could vaguely remember days when her mama *hadn't* laughed like that, when she'd seemed happier, when Maze was very young. Her earliest years, back in the mountains, were a blur,

but Maze did recall the months when they'd returned to the holler outside Torchlight, the summer Mamaw Marthie died—Vista
trying gamely to make a life for them there. But even as a child of
four and five, Maze could see the sadness in Vista's eyes, at the
edges of her mouth. The claw of loneliness already dug deep in
her heart.

The last time Vista had seemed truly happy was when they
had first come to Pleasant Hill, when they'd first lived there with
the Taylors—all that money and all that youth around them.
She'd wake Maze up early back in those days, to walk out into a
meadow behind the Deacons' Shop, the heads of wildflowers—
asters and goldenrod, a handful of black-eyed Susans—poking
through a blanket of early-morning fog. Never mind the long day
of work ahead back at the inn; Vista would prance through that
wet field like a young girl while Maze ran to keep up.

But that didn't last. Before long they were back in the mountains, then living with Sister Georgia, and Vista was spending all
her waking hours at work, or at some church meeting, all that effort
to fit in in Harrodsburg—the church committees and the choir, the
many jobs here and there, the divorced and widowed men who took
her to dinner at the country club. Working steadily, constantly, trying anything to dislodge that claw in her heart.

But Maze could see, if Vista herself couldn't, that none of it
was working. None of it could stave off Vista's deep loneliness, the
disappointment behind her sharp laughter, at the corners of her
eyes. Maybe her mama *had* been the one who'd taught Maze how
she did, and did *not*, want to live.

What Maze failed to notice, while she spoke in the student lounge that evening, was how the young men in the room started to sit up and listen, to shift a bit in their seats. What *was* a man supposed to do, graduating from college in Kentucky in 1963 with woodworking skills and a degree in philosophy and not much else, with a mysterious war starting up overseas, with nuclear bombs aimed at all their heads?

Dr. Wendt spoke up first, of course. "But didn't the Shakers take a vow of chastity or something along those lines—weren't they celibate? I thought that was how they died out in the first place. Except for the woman your mother cares for, of course," he said, nodding toward Maze. Dr. Wendt had a pretty young wife and two young children with a third one on the way, and a deep appreciation for "the ways of the flesh," he'd been known to announce in class, to the embarrassment of the freshman girls.

Phil and Sarabeth—who, Maze knew, had recently begun sleeping together—sat back in their seats on an old sofa, deflated, and Harris laughed and looked over at Maze in a way that made her blush and look away. "Well, maybe we wouldn't actually have to become Shakers," she said.

"That's good," Daniel said, "since most of us don't even believe in God."

Now Dr. Wendt was nodding. "You know," he said, "I could see this. I could see all of you making that work. A new utopia, grounded in different values. You'd be latter-day Thoreaus. Or the Vanderbilt Agrarians maybe, but without all that ugly nostalgia for the Old South."

That was the thing that always bothered Maze about Wendt—the way every idea had to be his. She only came to the fireside chats because Harris did. On the other hand, when Dr. Wendt got interested, it seemed like others in the room did, too.

No nostalgia for the Old South, no. Sister Georgia would never hear of that. Maze looked around the room, at all the white faces. Daniel would never actually join them, she thought. But what if she could persuade Mary Elizabeth somehow, to come for the summer even? Maze had never stopped hoping for that, imagining the four of them—she and Harris, Mary Elizabeth and Daniel—together, away from Berea somewhere. Or maybe there, in the town, but not students at the college anymore. Just weaving, building things out of wood, dancing. Mary Elizabeth playing the piano again.

Maze shook her head. Foolish dreaming, all of it. Mary Elizabeth had certainly made that clear. All she did now was study and check the mail every day for word from the University of Chicago. Foolish, Maze supposed, to think any of them would take her seriously.

But at the end of the term, when Daniel, Phil, and Sarabeth graduated and Maze withdrew from Berea, all five moved, along with Harris Whitman, into the old Shaker Inn at Pleasant Hill.

Squatters, some of the locals from Shakertown called them. Others called them communists, or worse. But still others, people who had known Maze since she was a child and watched her grow up at Pleasant Hill, brought them bread and cakes and pies and helped them repair the leaking roof and the broken windows.

Vista washed her hands of the whole thing and got an apartment in Harrodsburg. And Sister Georgia watched the bearded
boys and the girls in blue jeans, unloading Harris's old pickup
truck and carrying their boxes and suitcases into the old inn, with
a kind of wonder.

I t was the summer of her second visit to Pleasant Hill, a month
before she would leave for Chicago, when Mary Elizabeth began to take things. Small things, nothing all that valuable, but ob-
jects that would surely be missed. She kept them in a hand-stitched
muslin bag that she carried with her to Chicago in the fall of 1963.
Her second visit to Pleasant Hill was a brief one—only an afternoon. That was all the time she could afford away from housecleaning and caretaking in Richmond; she needed every penny
she could earn that summer for her move to Chicago in the fall.
Maze and Harris, Phil and Sarabeth, and Daniel had already
fixed themselves rooms in the old Shaker Inn and gotten to work
on a wide field behind the building. Mary Elizabeth saw Daniel
pushing an old handheld plow as she walked with Maze and Sister Georgia to the path to Holy Sinai's Plain. He looked up briefly
and gave a tentative wave.

Maze had been walking to Holy Sinai's Plain each day with
Sister Georgia, who'd grown frailer in the year since Mary Elizabeth had seen her. "I don't think she could do this on her own
anymore," Maze said while they watched the old woman run

through her daily worship, with considerably less fervor than the summer before.

"What's she think about all of you living here like this?" Mary Elizabeth said.

"I don't really know," Maze said, then looked over at Mary Elizabeth and smiled. "I guess you not movin' here with us makes you the only pure one left in her eyes."

Mary Elizabeth gave a hollow laugh but didn't look back at Maze.

Why wouldn't she come stay with them through the summer, at least? Maze had prodded back in May.

"Maze, I can't," Mary Elizabeth had said. "I've got too much to do at home." She hadn't said a word, though, about her mama, still in the Colored Home in Stanford. Or about the things Clarisa Pool had told her at Christmastime. For some reason she couldn't tell Maze any of it; she couldn't bear the thought of the girl's steady breath and her silence, or her stream of questions, or her sympathy.

She was hardly the pure one, Mary Elizabeth thought. Sometimes, that afternoon, when she caught Sister Georgia looking at her, she had an eerie feeling that the old woman knew that about her, knew there were secrets she was keeping. They all looked at her that way at Pleasant Hill—even Maze. Like maybe they felt she thought too highly of herself, with her big University of Chicago plans. Or, in Maze and Sister Georgia's case, almost as if they felt sorry for her.

"I can't see why you've turned so private," Maze had said to her as they packed up their room at the end of the year. And Mary Elizabeth had thought, Well, no, I'm sure you can't.

Harris could drive her over to Richmond for a visit one day, Maze had said, once they'd gotten settled at Pleasant Hill; how would that be? But Mary Elizabeth had said no, she didn't think so. Finally, to get Maze to leave her alone, she'd agreed to take the bus to Pleasant Hill one day in June.

Only Vista, who'd picked Mary Elizabeth up at the bus station and driven her to Pleasant Hill, seemed to approve of her plans.

"Good for you, Mary Elizabeth," she said as she pulled up alongside the Sisters' Shop. "You're gonna make somethin' of yourself. Unlike that lot," and she pointed behind her in the direction of the old Shaker Inn. "Lord knows what's gonna become of them. Probably a mess of babies before long, and that'll be the end of that."

She shook her head and lit a cigarette then, waving away Mary Elizabeth's offer of a dollar for gas. "Call me if he still can't get that pickup started later," she said. "I'll make sure you get to your bus on time." And then she drove away, without a word for Maze or Sister Georgia.

Mary Elizabeth was there for only a few hours, most of that time spent with Maze, who showed her around the moldy old Shaker Inn and told her about their plans to fix it up, along with the kitchen garden outside the Center Family Dwelling House and a woodworking shop for Harris in the old Brethren's

Shop. They sat at a picnic table in the shade behind the inn, next to an overgrown flower garden. The others—Harris and Daniel, Phil, Sarabeth—stopped by at various points to say a polite hello to Mary Elizabeth, then went back to their various chores.

When it was time to get Mary Elizabeth to the bus station in Harrodsburg, they walked to the Sisters' Shop so Mary Elizabeth could tell Sister Georgia good-bye. While Maze went to get Harris's pickup and Sister Georgia rested upstairs, Mary Elizabeth opened the trunk behind Sister Georgia's loom. Inside, she found piles of old Shaker books, including the ledger book from the summer before. She turned the pages, laughing quietly when she saw the recipe "For Sisters who have erred." In a corner of the trunk, wrapped in tissue paper, she found the stiff little bonnet Georgia had shown her the previous summer, saying she'd always imagined it as Sister Daphna's. Before she put back all the books and closed the lid of the trunk, for reasons that were inexplicable to her, Mary Elizabeth took the little bonnet out of its wrapping and tucked it into her purse.

Then, on a table beside the loom, next to a row of bobbins and a big basket of yarn, she saw the pattern Maze had sketched for the narrow piece she'd been working on at the loom; "child's blanket," it said in the corner. Hearing Harris's pickup, Mary Elizabeth started for the door, then stopped and hurried back to the table, grabbed the draft, and folded it into her purse as well. That one she took on Vista's behalf, she told herself, as she climbed into the cab of the truck.

Visitor

1947

Neither Taylor wanted dinner on the evening of their champagne-fueled celebration in the Shaker Inn. And the next morning at breakfast, Vista learned what she'd been invited to celebrate the day before when Russell announced that he and Nora would be leaving Pleasant Hill and moving to Philadelphia, where his father had several business interests that needed tending to.

"The inn hasn't exactly been a success, as you know, Vista," he said, speaking to her in the old familiar way—master to servant—as if he had no memory of what had happened the day before. "We'll pay you through the end of the month, to work at cleaning and packing up our things. But you'll need to look for other work now."

He cleared his throat then, and Vista feared, for a moment, that he was on the verge of saying something about that moment behind the Brethren's Shop. But all he said was "It's time I got Nora away from here; she hasn't done as well as we'd hoped here in the bluegrass." And then he left the table.

Later, as she cleared Russell's breakfast dishes, Vista wondered who that "we" who had hoped Nora might do better at
Pleasant Hill might be. There would be no way of finding out
from Nora, who did not come downstairs for the entire day, and
who spoke to Vista only in clipped tones, instructing her on what
was to be packed where and what was to stay, in the days that followed. At the end of three days of packing, she left for Louisville,
and Vista never saw her again.

Russell stayed on for several days after his wife's departure,
and what would surprise Vista most was how easily it happened—
how, after that one moment in the garden, the exchange of a single
glance as they passed each other on the stairway was all it took.
One moment she was filled with contempt for this arrogant man,
so cold and heartless in his dealings with others (including his
wife), so sure of his superior place in the world. And the next, as
he reached for her in the darkened hallway on the second floor,
she was prepared to go down on her knees and lick every part of
his thin, wiry body, stopping at nothing—practically panting to
be his new coal-country whore. If only to have him touch and lick
her back, for just that brief time, and to watch him lose his smug
composure and moan and shiver, both of them weaker in this urgent need than, Vista swore to herself each time, she would ever
let herself be again.

And so for three nights she allowed it to go on, for reasons
she could not quite understand; all she knew was an incredible
hunger, a longing that felt like a kind of pain. The first night he
entered her clumsily and finished his business so quickly that she

actually wanted to laugh. She crawled out from under him afterward and left him, sleeping soundly, to go scour her body in the bathtub and then crawl into bed beside Maze.

But the next night, and the night after that, he had had less to drink, and he took more time, and they tended to each other's bodies with an ardor that had nothing to do with fondness or affection; it was more akin to the greed of starving prisoners, Vista thought.

By the second morning, she ached, sore from the night before, but also troubled by this hunger that both shamed and thrilled her. During the days they barely spoke. In the morning, he packed valuable china and crystal into boxes; in the afternoon, he tended to unfinished business in Harrodsburg.

The third night, neither of them slept at all. On the third morning, he packed the Cadillac full of boxes and left Pleasant Hill for good. And all Vista could think of, then, was finding a way to leave, too.

She called Shade Nixon, but not to ask for her old job back. Instead she asked if he might consider going home to the mountains for a visit. She thought, she said, that she and Maze might stay there for a while. And she only heard the smallest, faintest hint of satisfaction in his voice when he told her how sorry he was to hear about the closing of the Shaker Inn, and that yes, he thought he could take a day off to drive her and Maze over to Torchlight.

Mamaw Marthie had not weathered their absence well. Holes in the cabin roof had gone unrepaired, and by the end of May she was still limping with her winter gout. When Vista asked her what on earth she'd been doing with the money Vista sent every month, if not at least hiring a neighbor boy to patch the roof, Mamaw pointed toward an envelope in a canning jar by the dry sink; it held nearly all that Vista had sent.

She shooed away Vista's fretting with a toss of her hand and eased herself slowly, painfully into her rocker. "I don't need so much, Visitor—it's better for y'all to hold on to that money." They stayed with her into the summer, and Vista got busy whipping her grandmother's garden into shape and bringing in two local boys to repair the roof and several rotting beams.

While Mamaw's face was mostly twisted now—with pain or with confusion, Vista was never sure—the one thing that could soften her gaze was the gold head of her great-granddaughter. And Maze did seem, if it was possible, to be turning even more golden. She loved the mountains, and the sun over Harmony Ridge in the mornings seemed to sweeten her freckles and make her blond curls even more radiant. When Vista asked her if she missed Pleasant Hill, her answer was a simple "I reckon. But it's nice here, too."

The old Victrola was still there, on its little table in a corner of the kitchen, untouched during the time that Vista and Maze had been away. At night they'd play some of the old records, mostly lively banjo and fiddle tunes like "Cindy" and "Foggy Mountain Breakdown." Some nights Berthie Dyer's twin grandsons, gangly fourteen-year-olds in old dungarees and bare feet, would join them, and Vista would teach her already graceful daughter and the twins, who were all arms and legs, some of the dances she remembered from years before.

They might have stayed even longer but for the lack of work there in Torchlight. And, though she hated to admit it, Vista missed the softness of the land to the west. She couldn't adjust to the *bleakness* of the place. People—whole families—packed into two-room cabins. Broken glass and rusted tin littering the dusty road through town. When she asked, she learned that the mobile library no longer came through Torchlight. Not since old Aunt Dawson, the only local user, had died the summer before. And the only men were either very young or very old. No one knew a thing about what had happened to Nicklaus Jansen. Vista no longer cared who laughed at her, behind her back, whenever she asked.

When Mamaw Marthie died, in her rocking chair on the cabin's porch, where she'd been sleeping through the August afternoon, it was Maze's idea to go back to Pleasant Hill. "Let's go see Sister Georgia," she said when they finished packing up Mamaw Marthie's few belongings.

Vista stared at her daughter. She certainly had no better ideas. She put the last box into the trunk of Shade Nixon's old Dodge, which he'd sold her for a song.

Vista slammed the trunk closed. "All right," she said, brushing dust from the car off her hands. "Let's go back and talk to Sister Georgia." Caring for a madwoman was, it seemed, the only thing left for her to do.

Pilgrim and Stranger

1963

There were other things in the muslin bag Mary Elizabeth took with her to Chicago in the fall: a pair of Aunt Paulie's lace knickers, which Mary Elizabeth had put aside and then stashed in her dresser drawer back when they'd pulled her aunt's trunk down from the attic to find a dress for Maze; these, Mary Elizabeth imagined, must have been purchased for Aunt Paulie back in Paris, by one of her many admirers. Also two of her daddy's cuff links, from two different pairs. A tarnished cross from a necklace belonging to Clarisa Pool. And a small, nearly empty notebook that had been her mama's. Mary Elizabeth had found it on a bright day in June, when her daddy had asked her to pack up some of her mama's warm-weather clothing to take over to the home in Stanford. Sarah wasn't any better than she'd been at Christmastime. She'd have to stay at the home a while longer, George Cox said.

Mary Elizabeth found the notebook at the back of her mama's dresser drawer, in there with her underwear and stockings.

Its old brown cover was stained and mildewed, and all its pages were blank except for rows of penciled squiggles on a few pages in the front and, near the end, four lines, each written in a shaky hand on its own page:

I been
I been there
I am
I am lost

Inside the front cover was her mama's maiden name, Sarah Henry. Written in ink, in a surer hand that looked, to Mary Elizabeth, like her Aunt Paulie's.

Some nights during her first quarter at the University of Chicago, Mary Elizabeth would pull her muslin bag of stolen goods from the back of a drawer and empty the items, one by one, onto her bed in the sterile dormitory where she lived in a single room. Eventually she would continue the ritual on her bed in a stuffy attic room on the top floor of an old Victorian house on a tree-lined Hyde Park street, where she moved at Christmastime that year.

This was the home of Octavia Price, the woman who taught Mary Elizabeth's introductory anthropology course that fall, and who took a special interest in her. She was a worldly, sophisticated black woman, clearly brilliant, and, unlike most other people at the University of Chicago, she dressed in vivid colors and long, flowing scarves. Her lips and fingernails were always painted a bright red, and her voice was deep and booming, her laugh loud and long. She had traveled all over the world and was, Mary Elizabeth decided, just like Aunt Paulie must have been when she was younger. She said this to Octavia, shyly, one afternoon in her office when they met to discuss a paper Mary Elizabeth was working on for her class. Octavia threw back her head and gave a husky laugh when she heard about an aunt in Paris in the 1920s, and her eyes glowed. "Tell me more about this flapper aunt of yours," she said.

At her big, ramshackle house near the university, Octavia was known to throw noisy dinner parties for her friends and a few of her favorite students. Rumor had it that she'd been married three times, once to a white man, and now her sometime lover was a man ten years younger than she, a jazz drummer named Marcus Dyer who was one of several boarders living in her house.

By December Mary Elizabeth was living there too, rent-free in exchange for feeding Octavia's innumerable cats and taking care of her plants whenever she was away. She planned to be away during the Christmas holidays that month, right after Mary Elizabeth moved in, and Mary Elizabeth said she would be glad to stay in the house.

Throughout the fall she had received letters from her father, filled with passages from the Bible and admonishments, which she certainly didn't need, to work hard and do her best. And also with repeated references to one particular widow from his church, Iris Jones—Iris had been by to wash the front-room curtains; Iris took care of most of the laundry; Iris had baked him a cake on his birthday. When Mary Elizabeth read her father's letters, she felt the long-gone pain between her shoulders return.

She wrote back to him dutifully, and every week she also sent a brief letter to her mother, mailed in care of Clarisa Pool. Occasionally Clarisa wrote back ("Your mama has a nice, sunny room now. She doesn't really need any new clothes. She sends you her love"), but her mama never wrote herself. She wouldn't even notice her absence at Christmas, Mary Elizabeth told herself.

Maze wrote to her, too, long, rambling letters that seemed to veer from happiness to sorrow to fear and all the way back again. They'd had a reasonable harvest and canned lots of tomatoes. Sister Georgia seemed weaker than ever but refused to see a doctor. November was cold, and the Shaker Inn was hard to heat, but they'd managed to keep the Sisters' Shop warm for her. What did Mary Elizabeth think about this war in Asia? She was worried for Harris and Daniel and Phil. Vista had split up with her divorcé boyfriend and bought her own house in Harrodsburg—how about that!

All of Maze's letters to Mary Elizabeth ended the same way: "Still wishing you'd come back."

In January Mary Elizabeth received an oddly terse note from Maze. She and Harris Whitman would be getting married, it said. Then, "Still wishing you could join us here at Pleasant Hill."

Mary Elizabeth seldom wrote back to Maze. She found it difficult to start those letters, and the ones she started she was seldom able to finish. The practiced, formal voice she used in her letters to her daddy and her mama would never work with Maze, she knew. Maze would be insulted.

Now, though, she would have to respond. But everything had changed, and she didn't know where to begin. *Congratulations, Maze!* she thought of writing. *And congratulations to me—I am no longer Sister Georgia's one pure girl!* Because since December, besides feeding her cats and watering her plants, Mary Elizabeth had been having sex with Octavia Price's sometime lover, Marcus Dyer.

It had started while Octavia was away at Christmastime but then continued after her return, every Tuesday and Thursday afternoon when she left to teach her classes. On those days Mary Elizabeth would race home from her own classes, and before Octavia had even packed her satchel and breezed out the door in a stream of silk scarves and perfume, she'd have begun to scrub the tub in the second-floor bathroom and run a deep bath, scented with Octavia's own silky bath salts. When she was sure Octavia was gone, Mary Elizabeth would sink down deep in that bath and sigh, and so begin the ritual of readying herself for the hungry eyes and muscled arms and probing tongue and cock of Marcus Dyer.

She would step out of that bath and powder herself carefully, but she was fighting a losing battle—her body was nothing but a pool of liquid need. Even its slickness and its smell could excite her. She'd wrap up in the kimono Marcus had brought her, purchased nearby, in Chinatown. It was how he had first seduced her, bringing her the package when Octavia left on Christmas day.

"Merry Christmas," he said and put it in front of her. She was sitting at Octavia's big, messy dining table, working on a paper.

"Open it up and put it on," he said then, leaning over her. "You need to wear something that's gonna let that soft skin breathe." His breath was warm at the back of her neck, and her hand shook as she put down her pencil and craned her neck to look back at him looking at her.

She did not flinch or look away. She was as hungry as he was—hungrier. She had waited, it suddenly seemed, all her life to feel that way. For all the shame and sneaking, Mary Elizabeth felt like she'd found her way home to something. What she'd found were Marcus Dyer's sleepy brown eyes and strong drummer's arms, his wide, callused hands and the slow, sure way he slipped her clothes off that first night, and the way he touched her all the other times after that—the smooth, perfect rhythm of the way he improvised on every eager part of her body.

When he left, to get ready to go out and play a gig, Mary Elizabeth would lie in her bed, smoking cigarette after cigarette. Eventually she would go back downstairs and fill the tub again, and this time she'd scrub and scrub, knowing full well she could never get clean. After that she'd go back to her little room and rip the sheets off her bed, and she'd pull out the muslin bag. One by one she'd take out the bag's contents and place each item on her bed: her daddy's cuff links, Clarisa Pole's tarnished cross, Sister Daphna's bonnet, Maze's draft for a baby's blanket, her mama's moldy notebook.

After she counted them all and returned them to the bag, she would go back downstairs to resume her studying at the dining room table. That was where Octavia always found her when she blew back into the house on a Tuesday or Thursday night.

She wasn't the old Mary Elizabeth, who Maze still wished would come join them at Pleasant Hill. That was what she wanted to tell Maze, but couldn't, in answer to her letter. So "Congratulations, Maze!" she wrote at the top of a piece of notebook paper. Then, "I wish you and Harris all the best." She folded it and addressed an envelope and mailed it the next day.

Pilgrim and Stranger

1964

In March Mary Elizabeth got another piece of mail she couldn't ignore—this time a telegram from her daddy, telling her that her mama was dead.

Somehow Sarah had gotten her hands on a bottle of phenobarbital tablets, Reverend Cox told Mary Elizabeth when he met her bus, and that was how she had managed to end her solitary suffering once and for all. Other than Mary Elizabeth, Reverend Cox, and Clarisa Pool, the only people at the quiet funeral service in Stanford were the head administrator of the Colored Home, two distant cousins of Mary Elizabeth's daddy—both older women that Mary Elizabeth had never before met and never saw again after the funeral—and Iris Jones.

Mary Elizabeth hated her daddy that day—hated what she saw as his rehearsed sadness, his excessive courtesy toward his two cousins, his smug paternalism toward the young preacher from the Baptist church in Stanford who led the service. The service, in particular, left a bitter taste on her tongue. What good had all those words of scripture ever done her mama? What good were they likely to do now?

At the cemetery, while her daddy wiped his seeping eyes and Clarisa Pool blew her nose repeatedly, Mary Elizabeth did not shed a tear. When her daddy returned to Richmond after hugging her tight and pressing several dollars into her palm, she collapsed on the sofa in Clarisa Pool's front room. And she stayed there for the next two days, staring at Clarisa's tiny black-and-white television and never even changing out of her pajamas. But still she did not cry.

Finally, on the day her daddy was to come to take her to breakfast and then to the bus station, Clarisa came to her with a small paper bag of her mother's things—a few lacey handkerchiefs, a pair of ruby earrings, some photographs of Mary Elizabeth as a baby and of her mama and daddy on their wedding day. Mary Elizabeth stared at the photographs, trying to find, in her blank baby eyes, or in her father's serious ones and her mother's shy, unreadable ones, some sense in it all.

Clarisa watched her closely. "They were happy for a time, Mary Elizabeth," she said, pulling off the quilt that was still wrapped around the girl's legs and starting to fold it. "Your daddy was good to her. He loved her the best way he could, and so did you. And now you aren't doin' anyone a lick of good spendin' your days here in my living room staring at the television set."

She took Mary Elizabeth's hands in hers and pulled her up to sit on the sofa, then sat down beside her. "She'd want you to get on with things now, you know that," she said. "You need to go ahead and get on with all you want to do."

Ten hours later, riding through northern Indiana on a flat and endless highway, Mary Elizabeth lurched to the back of the Greyhound bus, dumped the contents of the paper bag Clarisa had given her onto an empty seat, and vomited into the bag. When she got to Octavia's house at nine o'clock that night, no one seemed to be home.

Hours later she woke, in total darkness, to Marcus Dyer stroking her thighs and belly. "Shhh," he said when she jumped, and he reached between her legs. She pulled him to her then and reached for him desperately, telling him "Now," and then more urgently "*Now!*" until he was inside her at last and she could close her eyes and bite his shoulder so she wouldn't scream and only wish she could be like that, as lost to everything else as that, forever.

In the morning she took a bath, and then, back in her room, she pulled out the muslin bag and emptied it onto her bed, lining up the items one by one, counting them, touching each one in order. Then she put all of them back in the bag except for two: Maze's draft for a baby blanket and her mama's notebook. These she put into the tin waste can she kept below the sink in her room, and she lit a match and watched them burn.

Never once did her studies suffer. That was how adept she was, she thought, at fooling them, at appearing to be the same old Mary Elizabeth, the good and strong girl she'd been for Aunt Paulie and her parents. The one who was going to make a life for herself just like Octavia's. In the morning she rose early and left for the library. It was getting harder and harder for her to face Octavia, so she spent entire days on campus, returning only when she knew Octavia would be out. Not long after she returned from her mama's funeral, she began avoiding Marcus, too.

Later Mary Elizabeth would see how obvious it must have been to Octavia. She guessed, too, that Marcus might even have told her. Their relationship was like that, she knew; Octavia had other lovers, too. But when Mary Elizabeth realized she was pregnant, she couldn't imagine, at first, turning to Octavia for help.

When she knew for sure, she told Marcus, and when he pulled out his wallet and tried to hand her some money, she turned her back so he wouldn't see her tears. All she said was "I'll take care of it." That night she wrote a letter to Maze, asking her to get Sister Georgia to mix some of that nightshade tea, the one "For Sisters who have erred," and send it to her. That was how desperate she was, she would think only a week later, laughing bitterly to herself. Desperate and hysterical enough to believe in some kind of old Shaker voodoo, some backwoods abortifacient.

She mailed the letter the next morning, and when she returned from classes a week later, barely noticing the pale green buds that shimmered on the branches of the big old trees lining Olivia's block, there, on the front porch of Octavia's house, was someone Mary Elizabeth had never expected to see on the south side of Chicago. She knew it was Maze immediately, though her back was turned to Mary Elizabeth. She wore an old raincoat and muddy boots and held one of the cheap cardboard suitcases she'd brought to Berea, and she was standing on her toes to peer through the beveled glass of Octavia's front door.

"Maze!" Mary Elizabeth called up to her. "I never expected you to come all the way here yourself. . . ."

Maze turned around then, smiling, her face tired. And then, hurrying to the front steps, Mary Elizabeth got a better look and saw immediately that her friend was pregnant.

That woman—Mary Elizabeth's professor, the owner of the house where she lived—frightened Maze. Too big, too loud, too confident. She hadn't known any professors like that at Berea, not that she'd been overly fond of any of them, either.

"You said she reminded you of your Aunt Paulie, but I never pictured her lookin' anything like that," she said to Mary Elizabeth after dinner. They were up in her room, the evening Maze arrived with her nearly empty suitcase and the faintest hope that she might change Mary Elizabeth's mind.

"I didn't mean she looked like her," Mary Elizabeth said. She was lying in her bed with a cold cloth on her forehead. Maze sat next to her, barely fitting on the narrow space left on the bed. "I don't know why I said she reminded me of Aunt Paulie." Mary Elizabeth's lips were pale at the edges, and she looked like death, tossing fitfully on the bed and trying to find a comfortable way to lie.

"I was sick like this, too, at first," Maze said. "Sick as a dog, all day long. I kept thinkin', Why in God's name do they call it morning sickness? It's sickness all the damned day long."

She took the cloth from Mary Elizabeth's head, dipped it in a bowl of ice water she'd put on the table by the bed, wrung it out, and put it on her head again. "It gets better, though," she said, "eventually." Then she stopped herself.

Mary Elizabeth had opened her eyes and was staring at her like a caged animal. "I can't have a baby, Maze," she said. "You know I can't."

Maze could have kicked herself. She couldn't put off talking about the tea forever, but somehow she seemed to think that if she kept on making small talk, maybe she could. But small talk kept on ending up at the same place. Look at the two of them, she thought. What else did they have to talk about?

The bus ride up from Lexington had been miserable. Endless and miserable. By the time she got to Indianapolis, she had a sharp, stabbing pain that ran up her right side, from her ankle to her armpit, and no matter how she shifted in the crowded seat, she couldn't get comfortable. Sciatica. Vista'd had it, too, she'd said, when she was pregnant. But Maze wouldn't touch any of the herbal remedies Vista or Georgia tried to get down her. She didn't trust either of those disappointed women.

Now, at nearly eight months, she felt strong again most of the time, healthy and strong and ready for this baby. That was how she felt when she stepped off the bus; she willed herself to feel that way. She walked, wide-eyed, through the streets of Chicago until the sciatica went away. At one busy corner she found a policeman and asked him how to get to the University of Chicago.

He took one look at her and told her to get into his car. He dropped her right at Octavia Price's front door.

Mary Elizabeth shook her head in wonder when Maze told her. Then she pointed at Maze's giant belly and said, "How'd Sister Georgia and your mama take this news?"

"About the way you'd expect," Maze said, though that wasn't entirely true.

Vista wanted Maze to move into her place in Harrodsburg right away. She was convinced Harris Whitman would be gone before long. But they knew what they were doing, Maze told her. They got married by the county judge, and they listed Maze and their baby-to-be as dependents on Harris's updated Selective Service papers. Suddenly he was 3A, and deferred.

They also listed Sister Georgia. That had been Georgia's idea. She surprised Maze with that one, but then, it had been one surprise after another with Sister Georgia ever since Maze had moved back to Pleasant Hill.

No, there was no deed, Georgia had told Maze, not to her knowledge. Neither the land nor any of the buildings were hers to offer Maze and her friends. The Shakers didn't own things; they signed away all their earthly belongings when they joined. There was nothing she could do to ensure that they could stay. Unless, she said, they wanted to sign the covenant and live as members of the United Society of Believers in Christ's Second Appearing, as she had done. Maze shook her head at that; these friends weren't exactly the covenant-signing kind, she said. She didn't add, because she sensed she didn't need to, that four of the five of them were already breaking one of that society's cardinal rules.

Still, when she announced her pregnancy, Sister Georgia seemed surprised. "What'd she think you all were doin' over there in the Shaker Inn, buildin' chairs?" Vista said with her bitter laugh. But then, all of a sudden, Sister Georgia turned happy about the news—far happier, and far faster, than Vista. Once Maze and Harris were married, they could move into the Sisters' Shop with her, she said. She read the paper every day. She'd been worrying about those boys, about Harris and Daniel and Phil.

Maze told Mary Elizabeth all this and more when she arrived that afternoon, as they sat in Octavia's comfortable living room. She talked and talked and didn't stop, filling every pause, every quiet moment, with the sound of her own voice.

All to keep Mary Elizabeth from asking her about the tea. Because of course she had it, there in her suitcase. When Mary Elizabeth's letter came she'd gone right to Sister Georgia with the Sisters' ledger book in her hands, opened to the page they'd seen two years before. Georgia had a bit of everything drying up in the attic of the Sisters' Shop, Maze knew, probably including whatever part of the nightshade plant this unreadable recipe was calling for.

She handed Georgia the open ledger book, with Mary Elizabeth's letter on top of it. Two days later, Sister Georgia handed her a packet made from waxed paper, full of the tea.

"Use it all and brew one big pot," she said. "Have her drink just one big cupful first."

Maze had it, and she knew how to use it. But that didn't mean she planned to.

While she sat talking, about everything she could think of, the light in the crowded living room of that big old house turned dim. Neither Mary Elizabeth nor Maze stood to turn on a light. Before long the kitchen door opened, and in walked Octavia Price, in a blaze of light and color. She took one look at Maze and invited her and Mary Elizabeth into the kitchen for some soup and bread, which Maze accepted gratefully. She'd brought plenty of food on the bus—that, the tea, and one change of clothes were the only things in her suitcase. But now she was starving again, and tired, and happy for the interruption.

Halfway through her bowl of soup, Mary Elizabeth excused herself and ran upstairs. When she returned to the table a moment later, she pushed her bowl away weakly; her hand shook as she took a sip of water.

Octavia took a long drink of water from her own glass, looking over its rim from one girl to the other as she drank. Then she set the glass down slowly and held her hand on it for a while before looking over at Mary Elizabeth.

"I know someone to call if you'd like me to," she said, her voice measured and clear. "I can make the call first thing tomorrow and get you scheduled as soon as he can see you." Then she stood up from the table, gathered the bowls in one pile, and put them into the sink. "Your friend can sleep in the room next to yours," she said on her way out of the kitchen.

Mary Elizabeth seemed lighter after that. Still sick, but

lighter. But as Maze gathered ice water and a cloth for bathing Mary Elizabeth's head, Octavia's words slowly sank in, and she shivered with cold terror.

Up in Mary Elizabeth's room, she tried small talk again, at first. Then that "It'll get better"—the wrong thing to say, of course. She couldn't stand to see Mary Elizabeth looking at her that way. She closed her eyes for a moment, then looked at her friend and said it.

"You could have this baby with us, at Pleasant Hill."

Still Mary Elizabeth stared at her, her eyes grown even wider.

"I know Sister Georgia would welcome you, and we'd all be there to help. You'd be part of what we're tryin' to do there, Mary Elizabeth, what we're tryin' to build." This she was less certain of, but she said it anyway. The truth was that Phil and Sarabeth were already talking about leaving, and Daniel was more distant and secretive than ever.

Mary Elizabeth closed her own eyes then and shook her head. "Maze," she said, "please don't start." But she did start, both of them started, and then it was like they were right back at Berea, climbing the Devil's Slide or Fat Man's Misery, breathing hard around their words.

It's different at Pleasant Hill, M. E. It's nothing like Berea, and what we're makin' there won't be like anything else in the state of Kentucky.

Stop it, Maze.

You never even gave Daniel a chance, M. E.

A sharp, short laugh then, and a roll of her eyes. And I suppose Daniel's ready and waiting down there at Pleasant Hill for me and this black baby of mine to show up.

Is *that* what you think? You think you and your baby wouldn't be welcome there because you're *black?*

Stop it now, Maze. Stop. I have *classes* to finish, don't you see that? I have plans, and they aren't the same as *yours.* Why can't you understand that? Why haven't you ever been able to understand that? 'Wishing you were here with us' at the end of all your letters . . . when did I ever give you any idea that I wanted to be there in your little utopian homestead with you?

That silenced Maze. She heard Mary Elizabeth then, heard the resolve in her voice, the anger. Maze knew it was pointless to argue with her friend, had known it all along, really.

"All right, then," she said. "All right, M. E." She got up from the edge of the bed to hide her tears.

"I'm sorry, Maze," she heard Mary Elizabeth say, though she didn't sound particularly sorry. "It's just that I'm tired, I'm sick and tired and scared to death, and I have a *lot* I need to do." She sat up from the bed, steadying herself for just a moment before gathering a pile of books and notebooks from the floor.

"I'm going downstairs to study," she said. On her way to the stairs, she pointed to the room next door. "There's a bed for you in there," she said. "I believe it's all made up."

"M. E.? Just one more thing."

"Yes, Maze. What?" Like she was talking to a bothersome child.

"I saw Miz Price has a piano. Would you play the piano for me sometime before I go? Even just a few hymns?"

"I don't play the piano anymore, Maze. I don't have time. I don't even remember any of those old hymns." Mary Elizabeth started down the stairs, loaded down with books and papers, holding the rail to steady herself.

Later, while Mary Elizabeth studied, Maze took a pillow and blanket out of the room next door and arranged a place to sleep on the floor of Mary Elizabeth's room. She hadn't been able to sleep comfortably on a bed for weeks. In the morning she woke to the sound of a piece of paper being slid beneath Mary Elizabeth's door, inches from her face.

"Wednesday, 9 A.M.," it said. "Unmarked office on Halsted Street. I can take you there."

Maze sat up, the prickling fear moving up her sore neck. When Mary Elizabeth opened her eyes a few minutes later, Maze handed her the note.

"Don't do this, M. E.," she said. "I can make you the tea tonight."

When Mary Elizabeth left for class, Maze walked to the corner and found a pay phone to call Vista. Harris had gotten the pickup running again, Vista told her; he'd come get her when she was ready.

"Tell him I should be ready by noon tomorrow," she said, and she hung up the phone and cried.

The tea was dark, so dark it looked black against the red clay of the mug Maze handed her, and its odd, pungent smell reminded Mary Elizabeth of the front waiting room in old Doc Samson's house in Richmond when she was a child—a mix of earth and mint and chemical smells that seemed both to comfort and frighten her when her mama took her there for a sudden spell of diarrhea or the croup.

She drank the tea then, after a full day of classes and two rounds of vomiting and a supper of saltine crackers, at a diner down the street with Maze. But she drank it more on Maze's behalf than her own. By that time Mary Elizabeth was back in the world she'd come to know and want: a world of rational decisions and clear-cut medical procedures and getting on with business, a world with no room for Shaker voodoo like that tea she'd thought she wanted only a week before. There was a surer way of handling this problem than the mountain magic Maze was offering her, and she'd been foolish not to see that Octavia would be as clear-headed and straightforward about this as she was about everything else.

But there'd be no harm in drinking the thing, she thought; the worst it could do was put her to sleep, like the old valerian tea, and she was exhausted from the last day and a half with Maze. She'd already hurt Maze enough, she decided, and she choked down the whole bitter mug as she went over the notes from her European history class. Eventually the words began to run together on the page, and she dragged herself to her bed.

She did sleep then, for four hours straight, waking only to change into her nightgown and try to do some more studying for the exam she had the next day. She woke the following morning to a stabbing pain in her belly and thighs and a bloodied sheet, weaker and more exhausted than she'd ever felt in her life.

Maze stripped the bed, crying quietly the whole time, while Mary Elizabeth sat on the floor watching, hardly believing her eyes. Later Maze gathered up the sheets to take to a Laundromat near the campus. Mary Elizabeth walked to her class alongside Maze, leaning on her friend to steady herself and ignoring the stares of passersby.

At the door to the classroom where Mary Elizabeth would take her exam, Maze hugged her against her big belly, laughing through her tears as the baby gave a kick that both of them felt.

"M. E., why don't you let me get you back home and help you back into bed?" she said. But Mary Elizabeth said no, she could not afford to miss that exam.

"Good-bye, Maze," she whispered weakly. "And thank you."

After her exam, Mary Elizabeth walked gingerly back to Octavia's house, stopping every fifty yards or so to rest. Though she'd known Maze would be gone, it saddened her to walk into her empty room. But she was too exhausted to feel anything for long. She climbed into her bed and slept for the rest of the day.

That night she told Octavia that she had lost the baby that morning. So they would not need to go to the office at the unnamed address on Halsted Street.

Octavia only sighed, then nodded. "All right, then," she said. "Are you doing all right now? Do you need to see a doctor just the same?" When Mary Elizabeth said no, Octavia turned back to the stack of papers she was grading.

But Mary Elizabeth lingered behind her and finally mustered the courage to ask, "Did Marcus tell you? Is that how you knew?"

Octavia looked at her then, a little pityingly at first, Mary Elizabeth thought, but she quickly grew business-like.

"Why do you think he hasn't been around?" she said. "I told him to take his irresponsible self somewhere else." Pointing her pen at Mary Elizabeth, she said, "Don't even stop now, Mary Elizabeth. Move on. It's what men do all the time—you might as well learn to start doin' it yourself.

"And just be more careful from now on," she added as Mary Elizabeth turned to leave.

Pilgrim and Stranger

1965

Mary Elizabeth did very well on the exam she took the day after she drank the tea "For Sisters who have erred." She did well on all her exams that year and the following year, and she made plans to go on to do graduate work in anthropology, as her idol and mentor had done. She continued to live in Octavia's house, and when Marcus Dyer reappeared during her senior year, she slept with him again, a few times, on that narrow, sagging bed on the third floor. It wasn't the same somehow, though, maybe because she was no longer sharing him with Octavia.

Or maybe because she'd lost the sense, both horrifying and thrilling at the same time, of having a dirty, sullied soul that was making her give in to such urges. Neither a sullied one nor a pure one—despite what Sister Georgia might have thought. It was clear to Mary Elizabeth, who had barely spoken to her father and had banished any thoughts of her mother from her mind, that she had no soul at all.

But the summer after she graduated, as she got ready to join Octavia and several other graduate students for fieldwork in the French West Indies, she got a call from Maze, who told her Sister Georgia had died.

"She's already buried in the Shaker cemetery," Maze said. "But I want to have a separate memorial for her, up at Holy Sinai's Plain. I wondered if you might come."

She paused, and when Mary Elizabeth said nothing, she added quietly, "I'd like for you to meet our baby Marthie, too."

And suddenly, for reasons she did not let herself consider, Mary Elizabeth found herself longing to be in Kentucky one more time. "I'll find a way to get there," she said.

It hadn't gone the way she'd hoped. But still Maze had loved the brief moment of their experiment at Pleasant Hill. Patching the old roof and digging and planting and chasing errant chickens, swimming in the river in the late afternoons. Harris and Phil and Daniel made good farmers, she told them; they looked handsome with their tanned skin and untamed hair. She and Sarabeth drank beer after beer while they canned tomatoes one hot August afternoon, laughing over the two big pots of jars they ruined. In the winter they piled on layers of clothes to keep warm, and soon she knew she was pregnant. She'd promised to share her life with Harris without the slightest reservation; he was the one thing she knew about for sure. That was all their little experiment at Pleasant Hill had been, just one brief moment, and she could see that now. Sister Georgia helped her see it that way, and to feel better about it somehow.

"Your life is just beginning," she said when Maze came to her, crying and handing over the squirming girl Marthie for Georgia to hold. "For all of us," Georgia told her, "our time here has only been one brief moment."

The head of the county preservation society, a tall man named Samuel Dibbet who was sweating in his buttoned-up collar and tie, had arrived early that morning, Friday the 25th of June, 1965, to tell them they had one month to vacate the premises. Those were his words: "Vacate the premises." He added that a month was generous, in his opinion, for a bunch of war resisters who were living in sin.

Maze didn't tell Sister Georgia everything Samuel Dibbet had said that morning. The county owned the land now, he told them, since there was only one frail and feeble and clearly de-mented Shaker left. Arrangements had been made for her at the nursing home in Harrodsburg. The few other families left in Shakertown would be leaving soon, too. They should go back and ask their long-haired professors at that college about something called eminent domain if they needed more of an explanation.

When he drove away, Phil tried to make a joke about Dr. Wendt being bald, but no one laughed. Maze went inside the old inn to nurse the baby; then she walked over to the Sisters' Shop to tell Georgia.

They were going to make it into a place for tourists. Someone had already come out to ask Sister Georgia for any old Shaker records or artifacts she might have. "You can have whatever the young people don't want when I'm dead," Georgia had told the woman and sent her away.

They were already at work on most of the buildings. The Brethren's Shop and the Trustees' Office and the West Family Dwelling House had all been scraped and painted, the old reds, grays, and browns replaced with bright whites and pale yellows. For weeks now, work crews had pulled in early every morning, the roar of their engines and the buzz and whine of their saws piercing the clear air. The floors of the meetinghouse were polished and gleaming, the walls painted a clean, new white, the trim a muted blue. All the bundles of clothes and boxes of pots and pans that belonged to the Goodwill were gone, as was the old upright piano; the space inside was bare now, except for a row of benches along each wall—the way the preservation society members had determined the meetinghouse had looked during the Shaker community's most active period, more than a hundred years before.

Maze had to admit that it all looked beautiful. "You ought to go see the meetinghouse," she told Sister Georgia. "You could go in and have your worship in there." Maze still had the key, which, she'd discovered, still worked.

But Georgia refused to go see any of the restored buildings, even though every day through the spring and early summer, some other person from the preservation society showed up at the Sisters' Shop and tried to get her interested. Since the winter she'd rarely left the Sisters' Shop, and when the weather turned warm again in April she felt too tired, she told Maze, for the trek to Holy Sinai's Plain. She didn't feel the need to worship there, or anywhere else now, she said, and Maze didn't push her to say more.

But a week after Samuel Dibbet showed up and gave them a month to leave, Sister Georgia walked out of the Sisters' Shop with new energy, almost a spring in her step, carrying an old Shaker pillow made of a stitched-up square of muslin filled with the needles from a balsam fir.

She found Harris Whitman picking beans in the kitchen garden and asked him to help her walk down to a spot along the river she'd been remembering the past few days. She held his arm but hardly needed to, he said later; she'd scrambled along the path to the river like a young girl.

When they got to the spot she had in mind, Harris helped her get settled, seated on the ground, her balsam pillow at her back, leaning on the trunk of a paw-paw tree on the riverbank.

"That'll do fine," she said to Harris then. "You can go along back. I'd like to sit here by myself for a spell."

Did she need anything? he asked her, puzzled, but she said no, she had a flask of water in her pocket, and she'd be fine. She planned to think a while, maybe to pray. "You might check back in a few hours," she told him.

When Maze came to find her a couple of hours later, she thought at first that Sister Georgia was sleeping. She looked so peaceful there, now lying on the ground and curled up like a child, her head on the fragrant pillow. But she was dead, Maze realized before she touched her. Dead at ninety-three, with a funny, knowing little smile on her face. Maze sat down beside her and watched the slow-moving river for a while before she went to get Harris and Phil.

Mary Elizabeth borrowed Octavia's car for the trip. In Richmond she drank a cup of coffee with her daddy and Iris Jones, his new wife, in the front room of the little house on Big Hill Road. No time to stay for a meal, she told them; she was due at Sister Georgia's memorial up at Pleasant Hill in just a couple of hours, this was going to be a whirlwind trip, she had to drive back to Chicago the next day and leave the day after that for Martinique. But it was awfully nice to see them, she said.

After that it felt to Mary Elizabeth as if she didn't breathe until she had stepped into the car and started the engine, turned off Big Hill Road onto the highway, opened her window, and exhaled. She breathed all of it out the window then—Iris Jones's nervous banter, her daddy's bursting pride that made her want to spit coffee at him. Sarah Cox's presence no longer visible anywhere in that house, but her ghost there everywhere, everywhere Mary Elizabeth looked.

She drove fast with the window down, the hot wind blowing in on her, and she breathed in deep gulps of it. At one point it occurred to her to wonder who, if not her daddy, she had accomplished so much for, but she turned on the radio, loud, to get rid of that question.

When she got to Pleasant Hill she couldn't believe how much it had changed—all mowed and trimmed, with fresh paint on all the houses and buildings and not a soul in sight. She made her way to the Sisters' Shop and found Harris Whitman there, loading pieces of Sister Georgia's loom into the back of his pickup. He looked older than she remembered, with lines at the corners of his eyes now, but it suited him, she thought; he truly was a handsome man. He and Maze and the baby were moving back to his old apartment in Berea, he told her, for the time being.

"No place there for a loom this size, though," he said. "We'll just have to store it for now."

Mary Elizabeth thought, with a pang, of the draft for a baby blanket she'd taken two years before. Taken and burned, in fact. She'd thought of it early in the morning, as she'd packed her bag, and she wondered if Maze had started again, with a new pattern, and finished that blanket eventually.

Now Harris stepped down from the pickup and walked over to give her a hug. "They're already up there," he said. "I said I'd walk up with you when you got here."

When they reached the top of the hill, everything was bathed in a white-gold light—the worn ground, the circle of oaks and alders, the pair of tall firs, all of it the way Mary Elizabeth remembered it, and all of it glowing. And there, on the wide rock where Mary Elizabeth and Maze had sat to watch Sister Georgia at her worship, was Maze's baby girl. Little Marthie, a year old now, with a few wispy blond curls and dark eyes like her daddy's.

She was wriggling free from the arms of her grandmother, Vista, who laughed and ran after her.

When she saw Mary Elizabeth, Vista swept up the baby and came over to her. "It's good to see you, Mary Elizabeth," she said and held out her hand. She wore a trim pair of pedal-pushers and a pretty blue blouse, and her hair was neatly permed and set.

"Hello, Miz Jansen," Mary Elizabeth said, taking her hand, and then the child shook herself free again and tried to run, and then Maze was suddenly there, there and hugging her tight and crying on her neck, and then, to her own surprise, Mary Elizabeth was crying, too.

"I'm so glad you came," Maze whispered, still clutching her tight. "I thought I'd never see you here again."

Later, while Maze gathered together the things she'd brought up the hill for the memorial, Mary Elizabeth held Marthie's little hands while she kept on walking, in endless circles, around a deep hole Harris Whitman had dug in the middle of the clearing. Maze had filled a wooden box with various things of Georgia's— a ring that had been her mother's, some old books of poetry, several of the old Shaker *Spiritual Journals*, and, Mary Elizabeth saw, peering into the box, the Sisters' ledger book.

"No one but Sister Georgia knew about this sacred place called Holy Sinai's Plain," Maze said as they gathered around the box and the newly dug hole. "And if we can help it, no one ever will." Then she read a prayer from one of the dusty old books, and a part of a poem, Byron's "Childe Harold's Pilgrimage," that she said Georgia had loved.

"'On with the dance!'" Maze read, her long blond braid turning copper in the late-afternoon sun. "'Let joy be unconfin'd! No sleep till morn, when Youth and Pleasure meet, to chase the glowing hours with flying feet.'" Tears streamed down her face as she read.

When she'd finished reading, Maze closed the box and fastened its clasp, then set it down inside the deep hole. Phil stepped forward then, to help Harris fill the hole with the shoveled dirt. He waved to Mary Elizabeth, and she waved back to him, and then to Sarabeth, who'd arrived while Maze was reading the prayer and now stood behind her, watching. Only then did it occur to Mary Elizabeth to wonder where Daniel was. Later, while they ate ham sandwiches and potato salad in Vista's tidy little house in Harrodsburg, she asked Maze about him.

"He enlisted three months ago," Maze said as she wiped Marthie's mouth with a napkin, then handed her over to Vista. "He didn't tell us until just a few weeks ago, right before he left for basic training." She sat back in her chair and gazed out the window at the day's fading light. "He said it was the only responsible thing to do," she said, then turned back to face Mary Elizabeth. "I don't know. Daniel had funny notions about responsibility. Maybe even a death wish, Harris thinks, but I don't think that's it." She shrugged, then smiled sadly at Mary Elizabeth. "It hasn't been a very happy month around here, M. E.," she said.

Vista piled up their empty plates and carried them to the kitchen on one arm, lifting Marthie onto her hip with the other.

"Your mama looks good," Mary Elizabeth said, watching her. "Guess she's happy to be living in this new house."

Maze shrugged. "I don't know, M. E." She watched her mother collect more plates and cups, then turned back to Mary Elizabeth. "She loves Marthie, and she's finally got her own house and her yellow kitchen and all that, but I'm not sure any of that's made her happy, really."

She smiled, then laughed, remembering something.

"She doesn't really fit in here in Harrodsburg, you know, and I don't think she really wants to. She can't keep her mouth shut. Those county Preservation Society people had a funeral for Sister Georgia in the meetinghouse not long after she died. It was all wrong for Georgia, just a regular old Baptist service—she would have hated it. After the service, they had cake and coffee in the Trustees' Office, and some blue-haired woman said something about how seeing those flower children from Berea move in must've been what killed the poor old woman. Vista made a noise like a snake when she heard that, and then she said, clear as day, 'What killed her is what y'all are doin' to this place.'"

Maze shook her head. "I'll tell you, M. E., both those women—Sister Georgia *and* my mama—just kept on surprising me these last few months." There were tears in her eyes as she reached for Mary Elizabeth's hand and peered at her closely, probing. "And why haven't you told me anything about *your* mama for so long, M. E.?" she said. "How is she doin'?"

At that Mary Elizabeth looked at her watch and cleared her

throat. "That'll have to wait till another time, Maze," she said as she stood and drank a last sip of lemonade from her cup.

In the kitchen, Mary Elizabeth found old Uncle Shade, skinny and hobbling, a cigarette in one hand and a drink in the other, coughing into the sleeve of his sweater. He offered her a glass of bourbon, but she declined. "I still have to drive to Stanford tonight," she told him.

Before she left, she pulled from her purse the little Shaker bonnet she'd taken two years before. She'd thought, earlier, of sneaking back up to Holy Sinai's Plain while the others were heading back down the path and quickly burying it there herself, however shallowly, alongside Maze's box. But she'd decided against that, and now she brought it over to the corner of Vista's living room, where Maze sat in a rocking chair, nursing Marthie.

Marthie craned her neck to look at Mary Elizabeth but kept her mouth on Maze's nipple the whole time, working away. Mary Elizabeth laughed and held the stiff little bonnet out for the child to take in her hands. Then she reached for Maze's face, smoothing her hair with both her hands, then bending to kiss the top of her head and quickly turning to leave before she could see her friend's tears.

Sister

1965

Sister Georgia went to the river's edge to die. She was ninety-three years old by the clock of this world, barely a heartbeat, the blink of an eye in the realm of the spirit where she had chiefly dwelled.

Her life only one brief moment. Fifty years and then some at Pleasant Hill, yet she remembered the smell of camphor in her father's house as if she'd risen there that morning, as if the smell dwelled, still, on her clothing, the skin of her hands.

She brought along her balsam pillow, its faint scent of pine the smell of woodlands and of longing, and that was where she laid her head. Settling, as if into sleep—the settling of a weary body into well-earned sleep being one of her life's purest pleasures. Smell of balsam, also, sweet-sour taste of berries, little Maze handing her bouquets of weeds, the heft of the baby, Marthie, at her hip or on her lap. The softening, finally, of that stubborn woman Vista, who had, at Marthie's birth, finally let something loose, like air, like breath she'd held since her own daughter was born.

Then suddenly, in Georgia's ears, these words:

For seventy years and upwards
It has been my happy lot
To dwell with pure relations
Upon this sacred spot—

Sister Hortency's poem. Had she sung the words or only thought them? The sun was warm on her head, leaves stirring in a soft breeze, the river brown and slow, occasionally a bird's brief song trilling above her.

And then: *Lady Mar'gret she mounted on her milk-white steed, Lord William his dappled gray. . . .* And

Three times he kissed her snowy white breast
Three times he kissed her chin;
But when he kissed her clay-cold lips
His heart was broke within.

She heard it clearly and knew it immediately—that purest tenor, Tobias Jewell, singing to her below the magnolia tree.

She had spent fifty years hiding, she knew now, from the black-coated men who drove the engines of the world. Youth—she and Tobias, Maze and her young man and their friends—so powerless in the face of their laws and their wars. Yet children were born, Marthie among them, faces without masks and hearts still pure, their futures unknown.

One life only a single heartbeat. One blink of an eye. What was sin, or the flesh, in a vastness like this?

She heard the wind and the river. She could see Tobias Jewell's eyes quite clearly. She closed her own eyes and breathed in the smell of balsam, then sank into her well-earned sleep.

Pilgrim and Stranger
1965

The morning after Sister Georgia's memorial, Mary Elizabeth and Clarisa Pool were driving along narrow, rutted country roads outside Stanford. Clarisa had to be in Richmond for work at nine. When they turned onto the dirt road they were seeking, the only sound was the hum of the engine as the car bumped along. Nothing moved in the few tumbledown cabins they passed but a few chickens in the yards. A dog barely lifted its head as they passed a cabin about half a mile after the turn onto Black Pool Road, and Clarisa pointed out her open window to say, "That was your grandparents' place."

Mary Elizabeth glanced and nodded but kept her eyes on what there was of a road. When it finally petered out just before a stand of trees along a creek, Clarisa signaled for Mary Elizabeth to pull alongside the old fence to their right.

They stepped out of the car to the sound of one lonely bird singing. Beyond the fencerow was a field of clover, and the grass they stepped through was wet with dew. The sky was busy with gray clouds, rain about to fall any minute, and the green, living smell of the morning was too much suddenly, filling Mary Elizabeth's lungs until they hurt, until her heart was almost breaking. All she wanted was to get back in the car.

But Clarisa, even heavier now than she had been a year before, was already walking ahead of her, moving with dogged effort and concentration toward the row of trees, and Mary Elizabeth made herself fall into step behind her.

Then Clarisa stopped and pointed at a broad stump on the ground to her right. Its wood was gray, parts bleached almost white, and it was covered with tangled green vines.

"That's it," Clarisa said. "That's where it was. They cut that tree down two days after she found him. Thirty years ago now." She pulled a handkerchief from the pocket of her uniform and wiped her eyes and face.

Mary Elizabeth felt her knees start to give way, then straightened herself and took a breath. Strong and good, she thought— unbidden words—and she shook her head to banish them. The air was damp and humid, warm already, and sweat was rising on her forehead and on her sides. What was this thing in front of her? What did it mean for her to be here now, on some green back road deep in the Kentucky hills, trickle of stream down below, land no one bothered to farm now, grass and vine and clover without memory of that day? And a tree stump, also, she thought, without a memory of its own.

She felt she ought to say something but couldn't think of what. "Hard to imagine that old stump as a full-grown tree with a body hanging from it," she said, surprised by the flatness of her voice.

"Not really," Clarisa said, standing there beside her, looking ahead at the sky. "It's not hard to imagine that at all."

Later, after she dropped Clarisa Pool at the Stanford hospital, Mary Elizabeth grew uncontrollably cold, shaking as she drove. At the edge of town, she pulled to the side of the road, put her head down on the wheel, and wailed.

She didn't leave for Martinique the next day after all. Instead, two weeks later, she followed Marcus Dyer to Paris, where he knew some other musicians he could play with, and where he thought he might just try to wait out this goddamned war.

Sarah

1 9 6 3

One of them came to clean the house.

One of them took in the wash.

That same one fried an extra chicken the way George liked it every week and brought it to the house with some skillet bread and collards.

All those women crawling around the house like ants. Back when she was still living there, the only thing Sarah wouldn't let them touch was the piano. When she heard one playing a note or two, hitting the keys while she dusted, maybe, that roused Sarah Cox up and out of her bed fast, gathering a robe around her waist and running downstairs to slam the lid of the thing closed, hard.

That gave them something to talk about for months.

She felt proud of Mary Elizabeth when she wouldn't play for that room full of white men, but then sorry when the house grew quiet, the top of the piano covered with a thick layer of dust. She surprised herself by feeling glad to see the young friend who came for tea, the one with the strange name who asked her all those questions.

Why are you asking me about all these things? she'd wanted to ask the girl, though she tried to smile and give the shortest answers she could. Why don't you ask my daughter? But then Mary Elizabeth wouldn't know the answers. She knew next to nothing about Sarah's life before she was born. George had seen to that. Better to protect her from all that, he said.

So let's have your friend stay! We can find her a dress among Paulie's old things—let's get down that old trunk. And you go on to that dance with her, sure!

She tried to be the way a college girl's mother ought to be. But Mary Elizabeth said no, she'd rather stay home. Home with her. Her and all the ants crawling around that house, hoping to know their business.

Trouble come from music again. That was what her own mama would have said. Then that tea the girl brought home, whatever in God's name it was, the sweet way it made her head go foggy and her neck get limp, that easing down deep into a sleep that swallowed everything. As she drifted, she saw Robert and she heard his voice, still calling her. She spoke back in whispers until the darkness took her. But then the summer ended and the tea was gone, and Mary Elizabeth went back to college.

Gone again. No more piano, she'd said, never again.

Sarah tried again, but this time it was George who came and cut her down.

Then the busy ants were out of her sight and out of her hearing. Just old folks then, and the crazy screamers and mutterers—like her, she realized all of a sudden, and she would have laughed if she'd had the energy or strength.

She had no energy for anything now. She only waited for Robert to tell her what to do.

Clarisa Pool came every day. Yes, she remembered her, she'd tried to nod and smile. Old Win and Annie Pool's littlest one, a girl after all those boys, running after her brothers by the time she was four.

Sarah tried to smile at her. She'd been a skinny little girl with pigtails, and now here was this big woman in front of her, with tears in her eyes, eyes so deep and full of something. *Love and understanding.* The words came to her from somewhere—from George, she realized, from the Bible, the words he said every Sunday at the end of services: "And the peace of God, which passeth all understanding, shall keep your hearts and minds through Christ Jesus." But here in this woman's eyes was something else. *Love. Love that passeth all understanding.*

One day Clarisa Pool took her hand and put something there, a little bottle wrapped in a handkerchief. She put it there, and then she wrapped Sarah's fingers around it and squeezed her hand closed with both of hers. She looked deep into Sarah's eyes with her own eyes full of love that passed all human understanding.

"These are for you, for if you need them," she said. "You don't have to go the way he did."

Pilgrim and Stranger
1 9 6 8

Mary Elizabeth did not think of Paris as a city of light. For her, it was a city of shadow and rain, clouds of smoke above a plaintive saxophone, teasing notes on a piano, soft brushes against the top of Marcus's drums. Slow and smooth like that, a ripple of pleasure under the skin.

They'd parted ways not long after she arrived, but Mary Elizabeth stayed on in Paris for two more years, making her way and slowly, quietly, beginning to play the piano again. Here and there, in one friend's apartment or another, in the studio of a teacher who became her lover for a while. She followed that man to New York, another blue-gray city, and when he left to return to Paris, she stayed.

Her apartment, on the eighth floor of a gray building in upper Manhattan, was stripped and bare—white walls, wood floors, and a rich, dark rug from North Africa, sent to her from Paris by Marcus Dyer—who, she knew when it arrived, was hoping to worm his way back into her heart, not to mention her New York apartment. There was one piece of furniture in her front room, by a window that looked out onto Morningside Park: a baby grand piano. A used Steinway that had been a parting gift from her lover.

Most nights in her blue-gray New York City, Mary Elizabeth sat at that piano. She played Debussy again, and Chopin. And she started trying to tease her own songs from the keys, a little like blues, a little like the old hymns. In the morning, her fingers twitched and tingled the way they had years before, at Berea. In that other lifetime.

In Paris, she'd begun writing letters to Maze, ones she never mailed. It felt easier that way, from that distance, knowing she could decide later whether to send them. She wrote about herself, but also about her mama, everything Clarisa Pool had told her. What her mama saw, the way her life had gone at the end. The way she, Mary Elizabeth, had simply stayed away and pretended none of it was happening.

She did send Maze a card with her new address once she'd settled in New York. After that she got back a letter filled with sadness and regret. Daniel dead, twin sons born in a country that kept sending its boys off to die. It seemed, too, like Maze was somehow telling her good-bye. It surprised Mary Elizabeth, the fear in her heart at the thought of losing Maze.

When she got that letter, on a damp April morning with the smell of spring below the mist rising off the park, Mary Elizabeth put all the letters she had written in Paris into an envelope and mailed them to Maze. "There were things I didn't tell you, in

Chicago, even back at Berea," she said in a note clipped to the thick pile. "I regret that now."

She forgot to ask about the names Maze had given her twins, names she'd chosen, Maze had said, because they reminded her of Mary Elizabeth and her, that first fall at Berea—of their younger, freer selves. Pilgrim and Stranger, they were called, and Mary Elizabeth wondered which of the two was named for her.

Acknowledgments

First, a few words about the real Pleasant Hill and the real Berea College: There were no surviving Shakers (and no war-resisting squatters) at the time of the actual restoration of the Shaker community at Pleasant Hill—which, from all accounts, and as reflected in that stunning site today, was done lovingly and with great respect for the members of the United Society of Believers in Christ's Second Appearing. Berea College has been refreshingly frank about its history, including its actions as an institution during the years of Kentucky's Day Law. It is a college I admire deeply, one rooted, still, in the beliefs and principles of its abolitionist founder, John Fee. I am grateful to archivists and staff members at both of these beautiful places, particularly to Shannon Wilson, Special Collections and Archives Coordinator at Berea College, and to Larrie Curry, Curator at Pleasant Hill. All have been unfailingly helpful to me through the years.

Thanks are also due to Jan Russell-Urbani and Peter Christine for their weaving demonstrations and instruction; to Virginia

Wiles and Charles Rix for advice on all things piano, as well as a wonderful afternoon spent talking and listening to Charles's gorgeous playing; and to Ted Morgan for help with numbers and dates related to the war in Vietnam. Heartfelt thanks go to Gene Garber and Ursula Hegi for their continued support of this book through many years and many changes, and also to my agent Liv Blumer and my editor, Fred Ramey, Co-Publisher of Unbridled Books, for allowing me not to give up on Maze and Mary Elizabeth. Thanks also to the book's wonderful copy editor, Connie Oehring.

I am grateful for time and space provided by the Quaker retreat center at Pendle Hill, by the Vermont Studio Center, and by the Virginia Center for the Creative Arts. Thanks also to the Christopher Isherwood Foundation, and to Dean Gordon Weil, the English Department, and the Faculty Development and Research Committee at Moravian College for their support of my work.

Finally, I am thankful to my husband Jim and my daughter Anna, for their patience, devotion, and sustaining love.

THE TEXT OF THIS BOOK

IS SET IN ADOBE JENSEN.